# Serial Rain
# A Myrna Sontiago Novella Series


by Jameo D. Pollock


These rains bring more than water.

# Table of Contents

# Acknowledgments

Writing this book has been an incredible and exciting journey, and it would not have been possible without the support, encouragement, and inspiration of several people.

To my family and friends, thank you for your endless support and encouragement. Special thanks to Cynthia for the space to write and spend time with the characters in my head.

To my project managers, Zachary "Zack" Nelson and Zane Cooper, your keen eye, tweaks, recommendations, suggestions, and honest feedback helped shape the final version of this story into something better than I originally imagined. Your creativity, flexibility, and plans made it possible to get my book across the finish line.

To my beta readers across the land and dearest friends, Sakkuna Beach, Janice Curtis, Joyce Lapsley, Christina Morales, Zachery "Zack" Nelson, and Sue Saddington, thank you for taking the time to dive into this manuscript, offering your insights and pointing out the loose threads that needed tightening. Your thoughtful critiques were most helpful.

I also want to acknowledge Amazon KDP Publishing for believing in this story and giving it a chance to reach readers. Thanks for your support.

Finally, to my readers – without you, none of this would matter. Thank you for clicking on a nobody and sharing your most precious asset, your time, with my book. I sincerely hope with all my heart that I made it worth your time. This book is for you.

For those I may have missed, please charge it to my head and not my heart.

V/R

Jameo

Painting Pictures with My Words

# Principal Characters

**Myrna Sontiago:** Senior Detective, Homicide Squad

**Ezekial "Zeke" LaPorte:** Senior Detective, Homicide Squad

**Peter Bostwick:** Chief of Police

**Dr. Kathryn (Kate)** Price: Medical Examiner

**Tyler Stevens:** Information Technology Director

*"The rain will stop, the night will end, the hurt will fade.*

*Hope is never so lost that it can't be found."*

~ Ernest Hemingway

*"The more we value things outside our control, the less control we have."*

~ Marcus Aurelius

# Preface

Dear Reader,

Thank you for purchasing my book, Serial Rain: A Myrna Sontiago Novella. This is the second book in the series with Medical Silence being released in late 2024 to early 2025. I sincerely hope it provides enjoyment, excitement, and suspense as you continue to connect with Senior Detectives Myrna Sontiago and her partner, Ezekial "Zeke" LaPorte, as they traipse through Dallas. Happy reading to you.

Sincerely and respectfully,

Jameo D. Pollock

"Painting Pictures with My Words"

# 1 | ONE

The rhythmic back-and-forth swishing of the windshield wipers offered some comfort, but struggled to keep up with the heavy downpour of the relentless thunderstorm. Despite the wipers working at full speed, the windshield remained covered with a thick layer of water. The spring months in Dallas often brought frequent storms, and this particular one seemed particularly intense. The rain had been pounding the city for several hours.

The driver gripped the steering wheel and leaned closer to the windshield. Looking. Searching. This storm had been pummeling the area and created a perpetual cloak of darkness. He squinted, hoping it would improve his visibility and the likelihood that he would find what he was looking for. The intense wind rattled the vehicle, adding an extra layer of challenge to the already daunting task of navigating through the storm's wrath.

He was exhausted after driving in and around the city for the past several hours. Except for the blinding lightning strikes, deafening thunderclaps, and the splashing of water that his vehicle pushed out of the way, there's nothing much to see or hear farther than a few feet away.

Although he drives a 4-wheel drive diesel truck with dual tires, it's still dangerous to be on the road in this weather. Against his better judgment, he continued down the road. He would much rather be at home instead of out in this storm, but at least he enjoyed his job. Mostly.

He primarily works alone, which is fine by him. It's not that he hates people; they just make him sick. Figuratively, of course. Lately, they have been making him more sick than normal. Maybe it's because he was passed over for a promotion at work. Again. Or maybe he just detests people…their selfishness…their inconsideration for others. Then again, maybe he is weary of being ignored. Being invisible.

Sleepiness kicked in about an hour ago, but he must continue until he finds what he is looking for. He grabbed a thermos from the cup holder, spun the top off, and took a few long chugs of piping hot coffee. Hopefully, it wouldn't be too much longer, and then he could leave this nasty weather and return home. Even if he doesn't find it soon, he would still call it a day.

Up ahead, he could barely make out the blurry four-way flashers of a car. Unsure if it was stopped or moving slowly, he proceeded with extra caution. The vehicle appeared to sit on the side of the road, but he couldn't be too sure in this storm. It could just as easily be in the middle of the road, especially in the absence of any pavement markings. They're there but invisible under several inches of water and darkness.

The blinking lights came more into focus, and he eased off the accelerator. It didn't take much to slow the large truck, considering the volume of water collecting on the road and its speed of only 10 miles per hour. The truck coasted to a stop close to the motionless car. "That little car can't drive through this water," he thought. "Are they broken down? Or are they waiting for the storm to let up?"

After a pause, the man donned the hood of his rain jacket and exited the truck. The pool of water greeted him with a dramatic splash and submerged him ankle-deep. He noticed the gurgling of the storm drain as it struggled to remove the water from the surface. If not for his complete set of rain gear, he would have been instantly soaked.

He tightened the Velcro straps on his high-yellow, reflective vest, turned on his military-style LED flashlight and sloshed through the heavy current to the disabled vehicle. With a gloved hand, he tapped on the driver's window. The window, partially lowered, revealed a thirty-something female driver. He spoke loudly to compensate for the noisiness of the truck engine and the rain. "Everything okay?"

The young, curly-haired driver looked up. She whisked her short, ginger-colored hair back and shielded her eyes from a combination of the flashlight and rain. "My car just stopped. I turned the key, but it won't start."

"You probably got water in the engine."

"Will it start if I let it sit for a while?"

"Yeah, but that could be awhile. And it'll probably stall again driving through all this rain."

The driver slapped the steering wheel. "That's just great."

"What are you doing out in this storm anyhow?

"I'm embarrassed to say, but I thought I could make it home instead of waiting out the storm at work."

"I guess I can understand that. I am more than ready to get home myself." The man looked in both directions. "Have you called anyone yet?"

"No, it stalled, and then you pulled up."

"Okay. Let me see if I can get you going." The man turns to walk away but instead leans closer to the window. "By the way, what's your name? I at least like to know who I'm helping."

"Susan. Susan Jessup."

"Nice to meet you, Susan."

"What's yours?" she said.

"Me?" He smiled and reached into the pocket of his raincoat. "I'm nobody."

In one smooth motion, he drew a semi-automatic handgun and, without hesitation, shot her in the forehead. The rain and thunder provided more than enough background noise to drown the crack of the bullet.

The force of the bullet violently snapped her head backward. Her body slumped and slowly leaned toward the center console. The perforated, raised, symmetrical hole in her forehead resembled a small dark dot. Her hand acquiesced to gravity and fell from the steering wheel onto the gearshift as life left her body. Her head slowly drooped and rolled onto her right shoulder, revealing the gaping hole in the back. Blood ran profusely through her matted hair and down her neck like dark crimson oil. A combination of blood, brain matter, and cranium fragments speckled the dash, passenger seat, and window.

The man stared in disbelief. His chest heaved rapidly with labored breathing. His face slowly projected a smile quickly followed by a frown and back to a smile again. He would have loved nothing more than to stay and watch her continue to die, but he couldn't dawdle.

Satisfied with his work, he carefully returned the wet handgun to his jacket pocket, ensuring its concealment. He casted wary glances in both directions as he looked for any signs of unwanted attention or any unwanted traffic. He confirmed the absence of any prying eyes. Satisfied, he retraced his steps back to his idling truck.

He ascended the sturdy running board and found refuge within the shelter of the cab. Once inside, he allowed himself a moment to collect his composure, hands still trembling from the intensity of the recent events. With a deliberate motion, he peeled off his hood, revealing a mane of black and gray hair that clung to his forehead. As he secured the seatbelt, the subtle hum of the engine responded obediently to the pressure on the accelerator pedal. And just like that, the truck unhurriedly splashed around the car and gradually disappeared down the road, pushing further into the storm.

# 2 | TWO –
# A FEW HOURS EARLIER

Darkness blanketed the city sky despite the early hour, a consequence of the powerful thunderstorm that raged outside. The storm transformed the heavens into an ominous canvas of black, gray, and deep purple, heralding the arrival of tornado season. Each lightning strike resonated like a crash of cymbals. The wind added its own deafening baritone, howling in harmony with the elements. The rain drummed relentlessly on every surface, and the streets below were transformed into rivers of ankle-deep water.

Welcome to tornado season and to Dallas, Texas, located at the southernmost tip of Tornado Alley. Texas is the most tornado-prone state, with an average of 136 tornadoes each year, many of them hitting eastern Texas, including Dallas. The current superstorm, the first of the tornado season, exceeded expectations, carrying the promise of a violent and unpredictable tempest.

Susan Jessup found herself lost in thought as she stared out of the fourteenth-floor window of her workplace. She remained in a contemplative state, staring up into the abyss of the storm. It's early afternoon, although it looked like late night. Her head craned to look over her skyscraper neighbors that littered downtown Dallas.

Despite the formidable weather, she considered leaving the office, planning to face the thunderstorm, which seemed to have a serious case of anger issues. Her coworkers objected, but Susan was grappling with her own dilemma.

It wasn't an emergency. She didn't have pets, she's not married, and she's not currently dating after her recent breakup. The truth was, her anxiety was escalating, and the prospect of being at home felt more comforting than being stuck at work. She believed she could make it home before the storm worsened, as her residence was just about twenty minutes away— at least, under normal circumstances.

As if on cue, the office lights flickered, and after several ominous electrical clicks, they shut off, plunging the floor into complete darkness. Moments later, the emergency lights flickered to life, casting a limited glow across the space. Though it didn't cover as much of the floor as the regular lights, the emergency lighting offered a semblance of visibility, sparing Susan and her coworkers from the complete darkness that would have otherwise enveloped them.

Amid the uneasy atmosphere, one of Susan's coworkers took charge, drawing the attention of others. "Hey. Y'all listen to this." The workers gathered around as the volume on an emergency radio was increased. Following a few blasts of emergency tones, the broadcaster's voice broke through the static, providing a crucial link to the outside world.

---

"This is Vanessa Thompson for Dallas-Fort Worth Fox 5 News. An emergency declaration is in effect for the city of Dallas and surrounding counties. We are in the midst of a major, slow-moving supercell thunderstorm coming from the north, bringing with it wind gusts of up to 75 miles per hour, heavy rain, flooding, and hail. A tornado watch is in effect until 8 PM this evening.

The mayor is discouraging all nonessential travel until an all-clear has been given by the National Weather Service. For your safety, please seek shelter if you're outside. If you are inside, please remain inside and move to a sturdy location away from windows and doors. Stay tuned for more information on the storm."

---

Some of Susan's coworkers turned toward the stairwell. Others meandered into break rooms and filing rooms. She took a deep breath and slipped away from the gathering of her coworkers. She took the stairway exit that led to a daunting 14-story descent to the parking deck. The wind howled through the eerie darkness of the stairwell. She reassured herself that, at least, there wouldn't be much traffic given the severity of the storm.

Upon reaching the parking deck, she spotted her blue compact sedan; the familiar chirp echoed in response to the click of her key fob. She swiftly jumped into the car and dropped her purse onto the passenger seat. The storm's uproar muffled the sound of the slammed door. She secured her seatbelt, turned the ignition, and the engine roared to life.

She navigated out of the parking deck, only to be immediately engulfed by a deluge of rain and a violent gust of wind. The car rocked.

The windshield wipers struggled against the weight of the rain and the relentless force of the wind, limiting her visibility to a mere few feet. Despite cranking the wiper speed to the maximum, it provided little relief against the constant veil of water on the windshield. Undeterred, she carefully crept along through the flooded streets of downtown. The tops of the numerous skyscrapers disappeared into the dark, low-hanging clouds. Susan paid no attention, though. She was focused on her mission to get home, aiming to reach the highway that would lead her northeast of the city.

The sideways rain and hail created a symphony of sounds akin to machine gun fire as they relentlessly assaulted her car. Susan tightened her grip on the steering wheel and leaned closer to the windshield in the hope of improving her visibility. The onslaught of crosswinds bullied the vehicle, making it difficult for her to maintain control as if the gusts would easily hurl her off the road at any given moment.

The car fought through the rapidly rising water and navigated the inundated roads with the grace of a tortoise. She made a critical decision to take an exit, veering onto a secondary road that is now submerged in water. As she inched along, she reassured herself, "Halfway, I can make it."

The illusion of progress shattered as the ominous sound of stalling seeped into the passenger compartment. The car stuttered intermittently, and Susan pleaded with it as if her desperation could coax life back into the failing vehicle. "No, no, no, no, no," she yelled, her voice almost lost in the howling wind. "I'm so close."

Squinting against the rain-soaked windshield, Susan steered the car toward what she hoped was the edge of the road just as it gave a final cough and glided to a stop. She shifted the gear into park and turned the key, only to be met with a continuous whirring. Frantically, she twisted the key again, urging the car to cooperate. "Come on, come on," she implored, but the engine remained stubbornly silent.

Susan struck the steering wheel with the heel of her hand, venting her anguish with each muttered curse. The back of her head met the headrest with a forceful thud. Several minutes passed. She took a deep breath and pleaded with the lifeless vehicle once more. "Please start." After another attempt, the car remained unresponsive.

Defeated and isolated in the storm's wrath, Susan hung her head, aware that calling for help was pretty much an impractical option in this weather. Her parents, the only people she would consider calling, were out of the question. Her father, if alerted, would undoubtedly brave the storm to rescue her. Despondent, she activated her flashers and resigned herself to wait with no clue of how long.

# 3 | THREE

Rain relentlessly tapped the apartment window, creating a natural, therapeutic sound spa. Soft, distant thunder rumbled, adding an extra layer of ambiance. The atmospheric conditions would typically be perfect for a night of rest, except for the incessant intrusion of a ringing telephone. The sleeper tried to resist, knowing that answering it at this hour could only bring unwelcomed and bad news.

The digital clock on the nightstand displayed a bright blue '2:25 AM'. The lateness of the hour or the earliness of the morning always heralded bad news with nocturnal calls. She tried to ignore it but knew that she couldn't. Or shouldn't.

"It better not be her mom," she thought. "Always asking for more money from her dad's estate."

Her father passed away six years ago, and her mother seemed hell-bent on spending everything he left through traveling, gambling, and God knows what else. It's interesting that she knew her number when she needed help, more money, or when she was in trouble, but couldn't seem to remember it to check on her only child. What did he ever see in her? Myrna's characteristic impatience began to emerge, but she was working on it. Growing tired of the ringing and the futility of ignoring it, she finally acquiesced.

A hand emerged from the darkness, effortlessly finding the exact location of the phone, showcasing a well-practiced routine. Without sitting up, the occupant pressed the phone to their ear and emitted a groggy "Hello."

"Detective Sontiago?" inquired the voice on the other end.

"Ahem. Yeah. This is she."

"Sorry to wake you."

Sure you are, she thought. "What's up?"

"Someone's been murdered."

A brief stretch later, she asked, "Where?"

"North Ridge Road. Off I-20 near Glannaville."

"Okay. I'm on my way."

Myrna Sontiago ended the call but didn't return the phone to the charger. Staying in her cocoon under the covers, she contemplated the fleeting embrace of sleep. Unfortunately, expecting calls like this every night was one of the dubious joys of being a detective.

With a languid motion, she eased her legs over the edge of the bed. She savored the sensation of warm linens against her skin. As her bare feet contacted the floor, it was as if she was transitioning from one dream to another, the boundary between sleep and wakefulness blurred by the soft embrace of the night.

Outside, a distant rumble heralded the existence of the storm. A solitary flash of lightning danced through the slats of the mini blinds, casting fleeting shadows across the room. Pausing for a moment, she luxuriated in the quietude of the pre-dawn hours, relishing the opportunity to at least stretch and greet the new day, albeit not on her own terms.

With a resigned sigh, she reached out to switch on the lamp; its warm glow dispelled the remnants of the night's darkness. It's a familiar ritual, this interruption of her peaceful slumber, yet she accepted it with a grace born of necessity. After all, duty beckoned once more, its call insistent and unwavering.

Glancing over at the empty space beside her, she was reminded, not for the first time, that she was alone in the bed, as always. But there was no bitterness in the realization. There was only a quiet acceptance of the solitary path she walked on the road to her goal of becoming a top detective not only in Texas but at least nationally, if not internationally.

Myrna despised working crime scenes in the rain. It wasn't the rain itself that bothered her; it was the effect it had on the crime scene. The rain compromised evidence collection, especially during a heavy thunderstorm like the one that enveloped her apartment. Knowing time is of the essence, she moved swiftly.

She pulled her long, two-toned, brown-and-blonde hair into a ponytail, brushed her teeth, and washed her face as she prepared for the grueling task ahead. Her hazel eyes were still a little red, but she was satisfied with the quick freshening up. Opting for her trademark black pants and white top, despite their mismatch with her galoshes and hooded rain gear, she deemed herself ready for the day.

After strapping on her holster and securing her gun and badge, she opened the front door, only to be greeted by a face full of warm, wet rain spray propelled by the gusty wind. "Here we go," she mused. The journey into the stormy night began, a dedicated detective braving the elements to face God knows what on North Ridge Road.

# 4 | FOUR

The pulsating lights of police cars and ambulance casted eerie reflections off the low-hanging, ominous rain clouds. Even from miles away, they signaled to Myrna that the crime scene was drawing near even miles away. The rain, previously torrential, now dwindled to a gentle, persistent drizzle while gusts of wind stubbornly persisted. Ezekial LaPorte, her 37-year-old formidable partner, stood beside his beloved "Batmobile," a black Chevy Camaro ZL1, easily recognizable even in the dimly lit night. His towering 6-foot-4-inch, 250-plus-pound frame made him a commanding presence. The also 37-year-old Myrna, despite being a former track star at almost six feet tall herself, appeared decidedly average in stature when standing next to him. His close friends and coworkers called him Zeke. Others called him mister. Or sir.

As she caught sight of him, a genuine smile spread across her face, a reflection of the deep bond they shared after nearly 12 years of partnership. Their journey together had been marked by countless shared experiences, from the early days of training to the myriad schools they attended side by side. In many ways, they transcended mere colleagues, where they evolved into something akin to siblings, their connection woven with threads of mutual respect and understanding.

He served as her anchor in the tumultuous sea of their profession, a steady presence that grounded her when the waves of chaos threatened to overwhelm her. Like a Linus blanket, he provided comfort and reassurance, his presence a source of solace in times of uncertainty.

In contrast to her own fiery temperament, he embodied qualities of patience, kindness, and unwavering composure. His demeanor was a testament to the ancient wisdom of Stoicism, a philosophy that shaped his approach to life and work. She marveled at his ability to maintain his equanimity, even in the face of the pervasive specter of death that loomed over their profession.

Yet, beneath his stoic facade lay a heart scarred by tragedy. The loss of his father, a victim of senseless gang violence, weighed heavily upon him, a wound that refused to fully heal. Despite their best efforts, the perpetrators remained at large, their identities shrouded in the shadows of impunity. It's a burden he carried silently, his struggle hidden from all but those closest to him.

For him, faith had been both a beacon of hope and a source of profound doubt. The injustice of his father's untimely death had tested his beliefs, leaving him grappling with questions of purpose and meaning. Though he outwardly projected strength and resilience, inwardly, he wrestled with doubt and uncertainty, his faith shaken but not entirely forsaken.

And yet, despite the weight of his burdens, he remained steadfast in his commitment to their shared cause. His resilience was a testament to the depth of his character, a quiet strength that endured even in the darkest of times. Myrna found herself grateful for his unwavering presence, knowing that together, they were stronger than the sum of their parts.

Pulling up behind him, she navigated carefully to avoid the orange cones, taking in her surroundings. The unmarked road featured a grassy median with evenly spaced trees, dividing her lanes from the opposite ones. A lone gas station further up the road shone like a beacon in the night, while the other direction remained desolate.

Ankle-deep rainwater blanketed the road, and Myrna, still seated in her car, contemplated the likelihood of finding any lingering evidence. The grim reality set in – the chances were next to none.

Approaching Zeke, who stood near the flashing hazard lights, Myrna observed the scene. The partially rolled-down window revealed that water had already invaded the vehicle's interior. An officer valiantly held an umbrella, attempting to preserve whatever evidence remained, albeit likely in vain.

With a lingering Puerto Rican accent, Myrna greeted Zeke, "Good morning."

Zeke, towering over her, responded with a grin, raindrops glistening on his bald-shaved, caramel-complexioned head. "Gude mawrnin, Zoonshine, he said with his sharp Baton Rouge Creole accent.

Myrna chuckled, "Sunshine? Where?"

"Gude point."

Cutting straight to business, Myrna asked, "What's going on?"

"We have a young lady by the name of Susan Jessup with a gunshot to the head. She just turned 28. The coroner puts the time of death at around 7 PM last night," Zeke shared, checking his watch. "That's about eight hours ago."

Bending down to peer into the car, Myrna saw Susan's lifeless body slumped on the center console. The gruesome sight, with blood and cranium fragments, prompted her to think, "The bullet has to still be inside her."

Myrna moved to the other side of the car and shone her LED flashlight. She reflected on the tragedy. "Poor Susan. Who did this to you? And why?" She often referred to victims by their names, a habit she adopted after her father's death, a former forensic biologist. Her impatience, she attributed to her non-feeling mother, but that's another story.

"What else do we know?" Myrna asked, standing over the car.

"Thus far, no shell casings, but I would imagine the bullet is still in her head. We need to figure out if her killer opened the door and shot her or if she was shot after lowering her window. Either way, whoever killed her got pretty close before pulling the trigger."

Myrna nodded, considering the possibilities. "You think she knew her killer?"

"Not sure, but she had to at least trust them to allow them to get so close. It's evident that she was looking right at them."

"Yeah. That's why I'm guessing she rolled the window down. I mean, why would the killer open the door, shoot her, then roll the window down?"

"True. If that's how it happened, the killer may be very smart. Remember the Twin Killers? Maybe this killer wanted to use the rain to cover their tracks. Plus, if the killer opened the door, and she didn't know him, she probably would have been shot through her hand from being in a defensive position."

"Unless she knew him, trusted him, or he was quick on the draw. Has the 'crew' already taken pictures?"

"Yeah. I also already conducted a police call to see if we could find anything of note in the area. Why?"

"See if the car will start."

Zeke turned the key, but the car remained silent.

"I'm thinking that her car stalled, and someone stopped to help her."

"…or so she thought."

"That means we have the possibility of a random shooting of a stranded, trusting young lady looking for help."

"…or an intentional hit. Either way, we still don't have a why."

Myrna thanked the officer with the umbrella and gestured to the coroner that they could remove the body.

"We can have CSU check the car back at their lab once it dries out. Let's see what we can find out about Susan. Maybe that'll give us a hint because God knows this washed-out crime scene isn't giving us anything."

# 5 | FIVE

Zeke pulled the sleek Batmobile to a halt in front of the gray and white ranch-style house. The midday sun cast a muted glow after the recent departure of rain. The wet pavement glistened as the only lingering trace of the earlier downpour.

Gazing through the passenger window, Myrna exhaled a heavy sigh. "I hate this part."

Zeke merely nodded in silent agreement.

Informing the next-of-kin about a loved one's violent demise had never been Myrna's forte. The discomfort intensified now. Her empathy for the grieving family amplified the emotional weight. Memories flooded her mind; the unexpected call about her father's death resurfaced, the pain still fresh as if it happened yesterday. Each time she had to break the news to another family was akin to reliving that fateful moment, a wound that never fully healed.

Gratefully, Zeke's presence was a solace. He possessed a unique ability to establish rapport with unsuspecting families on the brink of grief. Interrupting Myrna's drift into the past, he queried, "You ready?"

"Huh? Oh, yeah. I'm ready."

Zeke, intuitive and perceptive, sensed Myrna's ongoing struggle with her father's death. Despite her outward facade of toughness, he detected the vulnerability beneath. While Myrna asserted that she was fine, Zeke recognized the difference between wanting to be okay and actually being okay. For now, he silently supported his sister-in-arms, knowing that sometimes strength lay in quiet companionship.

"You sure?" Zeke questioned.

"How do you do it?" asked Myrna.

"Do what?"

"How do you keep it all together? No matter what seems to be going on, you always seem so…so…"

Zeke interjected, "Equanimous?"

"What? No. I mean calm. And even more calm over the years. And what the hell is equanimous?"

Zeke laughed. "I'll answer the last question first. Equanimity is the state of being calm and balanced, especially in the midst of difficulty. Some call it being even-keeled. Special operator soldiers such as Army Rangers and Navy Seals must have it in addition to the ability to resist the fight, flight, or freeze response. Basically, it's the ability to not allow external circumstances to dictate internal responses."

"Okay," she replied, slowly holding the ending.

"The answer to the first question is a LOT of hard work and practice. In addition to lots of therapy when my dad died, I stumbled across a philosophy called Stoicism. I liked its focus and outlook."

"Of course, it had to be a philosophical approach," quipped Myrna. Most of us at the station refer to you as a philosopher, so this shouldn't surprise me. So, what is it about Stoicism that helps you so much?"

"Stoicism is an ancient philosophy that predates Christianity. Did you know that many early Christian leaders were converted Stoics? It has been practiced by kings, presidents, artists, writers and entrepreneurs, including Marcus Aurelius, the last good Roman emperor. It teaches people how to live well by focusing on what they can control and accepting what they cannot."

"That's it?"

"Well, it's more complex than this, but yes, that's the gist. The goal is to only spend energy on things we can control or influence. And for those things that we can't, we accept them as they are, not as we wish them to be."

"So, it's more about perspective?"

"Precisely."

Myrna slowly shook her head from side to side. "You're too smart for your own good, Zeke."

"Why thank you, but I am after wisdom more than smartness."

"What am I going to do with you? Are you ready to do this?"

"Yep. Let's go."

The walk up the sidewalk felt more like a journey of miles than mere feet for Myrna. Shaking off the lingering discomfort, she put on her game face.

A press of the doorbell button echoed a familiar "ding-dong" through the house. The door opened to reveal a small-framed, red-haired woman in her fifties. A single glance told Zeke that she must be Mrs. Jessup.

"Yes?" she inquired.

Glancing at Myrna, Zeke proceeded, "Yes, ma'am. I'm Detective LaPorte, and this is Detective Sontiago." He flashed his badge and identification. "We're looking for Mr. and Mrs. Jessup. Are they available?"

"I'm Mrs. Jessup. My husband's in the living room."

"May we come in?"

"Um. Okay. Sure."

As they stepped inside, Zeke and Myrna observed the house's interior and the family pictures adorning the walls. Mrs. Jessup led the way, and Zeke noticed a glass case with running trophies, suggesting a shared passion for fitness.

"Honey? These detectives are here to speak with us."

Mr. Jessup muted the television, stood, and joined his wife. Zeke stepped forward, introducing himself and Myrna before directing the couple to the couch. Before Zeke could start, Mr. Jessup took the initiative.

"What can we help you with, Detectives?"

"Yes, sir," Zeke responded. "Sir, ma'am, we're here about your daughter, Susan."

Mrs. Jessup's gaze shifted between her husband and Zeke. Her expression also shifted as the reality set in. She placed her head on her husband's shoulder, anticipating the impending heartbreak.

"I'm so very sorry to tell you, but Susan has passed away."

The anguished cries of Mrs. Jessup resonated through the house, followed by a scream of profound maternal grief. Mr. Jessup clung to denial a moment longer.

"What do you mean passed away?"

Before Zeke could answer, another question cut through the air in a strained whisper. "You mean…?"

"Yes, sir. Susan died during the storm."

"How?" Mr. Jessup queried.

"Was she in an accident?" asked Mrs. Jessup.

Zeke wished it were an accident, too, but the harsh truth remained.

"What was she doing out in the storm?" Mr. Jessup wondered aloud, clinging to the hope of an accidental death.

"It wasn't an accident, sir," Zeke stated, locking eyes with the grieving parents.

Mrs. Jessup lifted her head, confusion etched on her face. "I…I don't understand. You said she died in the storm."

Myrna, with emotional strength and tear-filled eyes, stepped in, "I am so sorry for the loss of Susan. I don't pretend to know what you're thinking and feeling. What I do know is that someone hurt her, and we want them in jail yesterday. Can you think of anyone that would want to hurt her?"

Zeke admired Myrna's ability to convey empathy while maintaining unwavering determination. An hour later, after tears of sadness and anger had been shed with the Jessups, the detectives emerged from the house, the weight of the news heavy on their shoulders. The investigation had only just begun, and the echoes of Susan's tragic end reverberated in the air.

# 6 | SIX

Medical Examiner Dr. Kathryn (Kate) Price found herself standing in the heart of her immaculately sterile examination room. The clinical ambiance was punctuated by the presence of Susan Jessup's lifeless body on one of the two gleaming stainless-steel tables. The molded plastic headrest cradled Susan's head, a stark reminder of the bullet that had been extracted and sent to ballistics for analysis.

Autopsies are usually routine for Kate, a methodical process of deciphering the stories the deceased can no longer share. Yet, occasionally, a victim slipped through the professional facade, tugging at the strings of her emotions. Susan, with her probable kindness and unassuming demeanor, had become one such victim. Kate couldn't help but see a potential daughter or son in her had she chosen to have children.

Kate methodically examined Susan's body. Her practiced hands scraped nails, combed through hair, and scrutinized under various lights. Despite her thoroughness, she encountered a frustrating absence of clues. The Crime Scene Unit, meticulous in their scouring of the crime scene, had already come up empty-handed. The relentless rain had purged any potential evidence outside the vehicle before their arrival. Even a detailed inspection in the dry confines of the CSU lab yielded nothing. The vehicle itself offered no insights; all evidence seemed confined to Susan's remains.

The ballistics lab, in their quest to identify the weapon, determined the bullet to be a 9MM, a common and inexpensive ammunition type in the U.S. Unfortunately, no matches surfaced in the National Integrated Ballistic Information Network (NIBIN) database. The type of gun remained a mystery, whether it be a Glock, Beretta, Heckler & Koch, Walther, or any other model.

Kate, seasoned by over fifteen years as a medical examiner, relied on her experience to fill in the blanks. The characteristics of the wound, the circular raised ridge, and the fragments around it spoke volumes. The proximity of the gunman, the size of the bullet, and the lack of exit suggested a low-velocity shot. Susan shot from a mere four feet or less, suffered massive blood loss and a devastating brain injury. The projectile tore through her cranium, leaving a penetrating wound and a permanent cavity, with a shockwave creating a knife-like wound in the back of her head.

Left with nothing tangible beyond the evident, Kate prepared to place Susan's body in the mortuary refrigerator at a chilling 36 degrees until Myrna and Zeke authorized its release to the grieving family. Stepping into the adjacent prep room, she glanced once more at Susan through the window before shedding her surgical garb. Dialing a familiar extension from memory, she contacted her assistants.

"Yes, Dr. Price?" answered a voice on the other end of the line.

"Would you and the intern move Ms. Jessup to the cooler, please?" Kate requested, her tone professional but tinged with a hint of weariness.

"Sure. Be there in just a sec," came the reply.

Hanging up the phone, Kate took a moment to collect her thoughts. She reflected on the weight of her responsibilities, the emotional toll of dealing with lives cut short, and the perpetual search for answers in the face of seemingly insurmountable challenges. She knew that every piece of evidence, every detail, no matter how small, could be the key to solving the puzzle of Susan's untimely death.

As her assistants arrived to move Susan's body, Kate watched them with a critical eye, ensuring they handled the transfer with the utmost care and respect. The stainless-steel table glistened under the harsh fluorescent lights, now empty and waiting for the next case. In this room, life and death intersect in the most tangible ways, and Kate is acutely aware of her role as the intermediary.

With Susan's body safely stored in the cooler, Kate returned to her desk, where a mountain of paperwork awaited her. She knew that Myrna and Zeke were out there, tirelessly working to find the killer. Their dedication fueled her own, reminding her that every autopsy, every report, and every minute spent in that room was a step closer to justice for Susan and all the others who had met similar fates.

As the hours ticked by, her focus never wavered. She meticulously documented her findings, knowing that her report would be crucial in the investigation. Each detail, each observation, was another piece of the puzzle that would hopefully lead to the capture of a murderer.

# 7 | SEVEN

The late evening enveloped the Batmobile as it navigated the illuminated expanse of downtown Dallas. The city's skyline was a glittering backdrop against the dark, rain-soaked sky. Myrna and Zeke were on their way back to the precinct after a follow-up visit to Susan's workplace. The day was drenched not just in the persistent rain but also in the frustrating lack of evidence. The downpour, though heavy, didn't rival the ferocity of the earlier storm in the week, which had left the streets flooded and chaotic. The water had risen quickly, causing traffic jams and even a few minor accidents. The aftermath was still evident in the scattered debris and lingering puddles.

Several days had elapsed since Susan's tragic demise, and the elusive trail leading to her killer remained as slippery as the rain-slicked streets. The evidence-gods had withheld any leads on a potential boyfriend, husband, recent ex, or work-related troubles. Even Susan's best friend, whose interview ended at another dead end, provided no insights. All accounts of Susan emphasized her kindness, helpful nature, and proficiency as an accountant but offered no hint of any tumultuous undercurrents in her life. Her colleagues spoke highly of her, describing her as someone who always went the extra mile, both in her professional duties and her personal relationships. She was well-liked, and no one could fathom why anyone would want to harm her.

In the confines of the Batmobile, Myrna broke the silence with a sigh. "I'm all for April showers, but Spring in Dallas is beginning to get me down," she murmured, her voice reflecting her frustration. The constant rain seemed to mirror the relentless dead ends they kept encountering.

"I love the rain," Zeke replied, his gaze steady on the road, the wipers working overtime to clear the windshield. "It feels like it washes away the grime of the city. Plus, it brings a certain peace, don't you think?"

"I don't hate it, but these next few months will be filled with nothing but rain," Myrna retorted, looking out at the rain-drenched cityscape. The endless gray skies and waterlogged streets were starting to wear on her spirits.

"But just think, it only rains about nine days a month during this time of year," Zeke said, always ready with a statistic. He loved finding little facts about their city, especially those that others might overlook.

"I should have known you would have a statistic hiding somewhere, Mr. Trivia," Myrna teased, rolling her eyes. It was just like Zeke to try to find a silver lining in everything.

"I'm just curious about our city," Zeke responded with a grin, his eyes momentarily flicked towards Myrna before returning to the road. "It's part of its charm."

"Sure, you are," Myrna said, a smile tugging at her lips. Despite the bleakness of the day, Zeke's optimism was contagious.

Myrna's fingers danced on her phone as she browsed information. A moment later, she smiled and turned to Zeke. "Did you know that

Dallas gets three to five inches of rainfall during the Spring months?" she asked, her curiosity piqued by the trivia she'd just discovered.

Zeke shot a curious glance toward Myrna. "Yep. Did you?"

"Of course, that's why I asked you," she replied with a smirk. She knew he probably had the answer ready even before she asked.

"Turn your phone this way," Zeke insisted, clearly interested in what she'd found.

"That's okay. I'm good," Myrna said, holding her phone protectively. She enjoyed teasing him with little bits of information she knew he would find fascinating.

"That's what I thought," Zeke chuckled, shaking his head. Their playful banter was a welcome distraction from the heavy thoughts that usually occupied their minds.

Their banter, punctuated by a brief shared laugh, was cut short as Myrna's phone chirped with an incoming call. She swiped the screen to answer, her expression shifting as she listened intently. Zeke, sensing a shift in the atmosphere, eased off the accelerator, preparing for what would come next. The tension in the car became palpable as Myrna processed the information.

"Where? Okay, thanks. We're on our way," Myrna stated before ending the call. Her tone was clipped, indicating the seriousness of the situation.

"Where're we on our way to?" Zeke inquired, his focus shifting gears. He could tell from Myrna's expression that it was something urgent.

"West Side. On the outskirts of the historic district," Myrna answered, her tone serious. The location brought back memories neither of them were eager to revisit.

Before they could make the turn to the underground parking deck of police headquarters, Zeke activated the blue lights, executed a swift U-turn, and accelerated with purpose. The siren cut through the rain, drawing the attention of pedestrians and other drivers. They needed to get there as quickly as possible.

Myrna's gaze wandered out the passenger window, the city's buildings blurring past. The historic district loomed ahead, a place that held memories of the grim discovery of Jenni's lifeless body.

The haunting image of Jenni, a fellow detective's wife, hung upside down and spread-eagle on the abandoned Dallas High School, flashed in Myrna's mind. It was a stark reminder of the weight of failure she felt at that moment. It happened a few years ago, but it was still ever present in her mind. The trauma of that case had left a lasting scar on her psyche.

Shaking off the haunting memories, she refocused on the road ahead, steeling herself for the challenges the West Side may hold.

# 8 | EIGHT

The steady stream of rain created a rhythmic drumming against the canvas of flashing police lights. The setting was a somber tone for the grim scene awaiting the detectives. Uniformed police officers had cordoned off the area with cones, guiding curious onlookers and managing the traffic eager to witness the unfolding drama. The atmosphere was thick with tension and the scent of wet pavement.

Zeke brought the Batmobile to a halt, and a moment of contemplation passed before he pressed a button on the dashboard. A metallic thunk resonated from the rear of the sleek vehicle as he retrieved rain jackets, surprising Myrna by producing one for her as well. The rain had intensified, creating a continuous curtain of water that blurred the edges of the scene.

A sly grin formed on Zeke's face as he handed over the jacket. "Batman is always prepared," he quipped, the tension easing slightly with his humor.

Myrna playfully shook her head accepting the jacket. "Don't you think you're a little too big to be Batman?" she teased, the light-hearted banter, a momentary escape from the gravity of their task.

Zeke chuckled, the sound blending with the patter of rain. "Me? Of course not. Batmans got nothing on me," he retorted, his broad shoulders filling the jacket impressively.

Raindrops and the sound of splashing footsteps created the only symphony as they made their way to the crime scene. Myrna couldn't help but notice the unsettling parallels to the last murder – another stranded vehicle, a partially lowered window, and a lifeless driver. The haunting thought lingered: *"I hope this isn't another gunshot to the head."* She felt a shiver, not from the cold but from the eerie similarity.

She walked around the gold-colored sedan, meticulously scanning for anything out of place. The right front tire was flat, adding a detail that might be crucial. Her rain jacket offered some protection, but her hair was thoroughly soaked. She absentmindedly ran her fingers through the damp strands – a habitual sign of her self-imposed frustration and concentration.

Her circuit around the vehicle concluded next to Zeke at the driver's side door. They shared a moment of silent communication through a brief glance. Zeke nodded, and with caution, he opened the door, mindful of preserving potential evidence. The interior light flickered on, casting a stark glow on the grim scene inside.

The elderly man lay on the bench seat, forced to one side by the impact of the fatal shot. A crushed fedora lay beneath him, and a blood-spattered newspaper adorned the passenger side floorboard. The interior was eerily silent, a soundscape of death. Blood spray covered the surfaces. It was a stark contrast to the rain's constant drizzle on the roof and windshield. The scene was almost surreal in its quiet horror.

With the absence of a weapon, shell casings, or any evidence beyond the gruesome scene, Myrna noted a few key differences from the last case. The victim was an elderly man, and the flat tire added a new layer to the mystery. The gunshot wound, more devastating than the previous one, suggested a higher caliber or velocity bullet, possibly indicating a closer range. The details began to form a troubling picture in her mind.

Myrna turned to Zeke, her voice cutting through the rain. "We got a name?" she asked, hoping for a lead.

The responding officer stepped forward; his uniform soaked through. "We didn't check for a wallet, but the vehicle's registered to a Mr. Arnold Jessup, 72 years old, from Plano. He certainly fits the description," he reported, handing over the registration details.

Observing Zeke scribbling notes, Myrna asked, "Any thoughts?" Her voice was steady, but her mind raced with possibilities.

Zeke looked up; raindrops speckled his notepad. "Yeah. I'm thinking that except for a few differences, this looks just like the last scene," he said, his tone grim.

"Me, too," Myrna agreed, the similarities unnerving her.

"You know what they say. Once is an accident. Twice is a coincidence—"

"—third time's a pattern," Myrna finished, their synergy evident. The words hung in the air, heavy with implication.

"Yep. It looks like a higher-caliber bullet, though. You think we have two shooters?" Zeke mused, considering the possibility.

"I wouldn't rule it out. I just hope that this isn't the beginning of something, but it sure looks like it. I mean, what are the chances that two unsuspecting drivers with car trouble are murdered with a single gunshot to the head?" Myrna's voice carried a note of dread.

"Unfortunately, I have to agree. We may be dealing with a reverse good Samaritan," Zeke speculated, the term sending a chill through them both.

"Or a disgruntled tow truck driver rolling around town. Let's go talk to the family and see what we can learn before someone else dies and these shootings become a pattern. Then we could check the local towing companies to see if they received a call from either of our victims," Myrna suggested, her mind already forming a plan of action.

As they turned to leave, the rain continued to pour, relentless and unyielding. Within the Batmobile, the sense of resolve intensified. They knew that the night was, unfortunately, far from over.

# 9 | NINE

Zeke lightly tapped on the partially opened door to Kate's basement office; his knuckles barely made a sound on the wooden frame. "You here, Kate?" he asked, peering inside the dimly lit room, his voice echoing slightly.

"Perfect timing," came Kate's voice from behind the door. "Come in if you can squeeze through."

Zeke pushed the door open wider and surveyed the cramped space. Her office resembled a closet more than an office, with filing cabinets and papers stacked high. However, the three of them managed to squeeze in, closing the door behind them with some difficulty.

"I'll get right to the point," Kate began. "The bullet that killed Mr. Mallard is different from the one used on Susan. It was a 'man-stopper'."

Myrna's eyes widened in shock. "What?"

Zeke shook his head, understanding the gravity of the situation. "Hollow-point bullets on steroids," he explained.

"Man-stopper bullets, also called one-shot man-stoppers, are lead bullets that look more like a small socket from a toolbox than a bullet," Kate elaborated. "They come in different calibers but are commonly used in the .38 special family. The 'man-stopper' is well beyond the ammunition permitted for use by law enforcement."

Kate added, "Yeah. It also over-penetrates, expands once inside, and rarely exits. It's designed for maximum punishment and maximum damage, and it did its job with Mr. Mallard, evidenced by the huge hole in the back of his head. You don't even want to know what the inside of his head looked like."

"So, not only are they killing innocent people, but they're also making their bullets, too," said Myrna, her voice tinged with disbelief.

A heavy silence filled the room; the weight of the information settled over them like a dark cloud. Myrna finally broke the silence and turned her attention to Kate. "I was asked earlier if I think we're dealing with one shooter. What's your take on it?"

"Good question," replied Kate, considering the possibilities. "I don't subscribe to coincidences. However, there are too many not to assume that you're dealing with only one lunatic."

"That's what I was thinking. Two different bullets, same M.O.," said Myrna, "but why change the ammunition, especially since the other one was plenty effective?"

"Maybe the point is to have us think there are multiple shooters," suggested Zeke. "But if he were as smart as he—or she—thinks they are, they would know that the same M.O. would connect the shootings."

"True, but we definitely can't rule out more than one, though," Myrna said thoughtfully.

Zeke rubbed his lower back, the old injury still giving him trouble. "Yeah, especially with what we had to deal with a few years ago."

"Yeah," said Myrna, "that was a hard lesson, but I've learned not to assume anything anymore."

Last year, Myrna and Zeke tracked a serial killer to his residence as he was preparing to torture and kill a young teenage boy. Myrna had shot and killed the killer, but not before he managed to shoot Zeke in the back. Her impatience had gotten the better of her, and she left Zeke uncovered to check the rest of the house while he freed the boy. Unbeknownst to either of them, the killer was hiding in a secret room in the basement. She returned just as the killer took his shot at Zeke. She had feared he wouldn't survive.

While Zeke was in the ICU, another person had been killed in the same manner as the others. Their first thought was that it was a copycat or an undiscovered body that had been planted earlier. It had never dawned on her that there were two killers. Not only were they brothers, but they were also identical twins. Since then, she had learned not to dismiss any idea, regardless of how far-fetched it might initially seem. She also knew she needed to control her impatience better.

Myrna shuddered at the memory. "Thanks, Kate. Let us know if you think of anything else that can help us."

"Don't I always?" Kate replied with a small smile.

"Well, Zeke," said Myrna, turning to her partner, "I guess it's time to bring the Chief up to speed."

# 10 | TEN

After a grueling thirteen-hour shift that stretched from the early hours of eight in the morning to the evening shadows at nine, Brad found himself yearning for the sanctuary of his home. The long hours had taken their toll, and the comfort of his own space felt like a distant yet tantalizing promise. His drive home marked the end of a day saturated with responding to accidents, overdoses, and urgent calls of medical emergencies. The relentless rain, a fitting backdrop to the last half of his demanding shift, now clung to the cityscape, turning the streets into a glossy, reflective surface that mirrored the exhaustion etched on his face. The rain threatened to persist into the early morning when he would once again be at the mercy of the work clock, facing another round of unpredictable and relentless emergencies. The drive, though familiar, felt like a journey through a blurred world, each raindrop a tiny mirror reflecting the fatigue that had settled deep into his bones.

Although the time frame from eight to nine in the evening might seem reasonable to some, the weight of thirteen hours spent immersed in a whirlwind of medical crises could not be overstated. Each minute stretched into an eternity as he navigated through one high-stress situation after another. Fatigue permeated his every fiber. The prospect of unwinding with a book or catching up on a favorite show seemed increasingly unlikely as the reality of his exhaustion settled in. The anticipation of a quiet evening at home felt like a cruel mirage, tantalizingly close yet achingly out of reach.

As he navigated away from the bustling cityscape, he veered off the interstate into the rural expanse of Dallas. The transition from urban chaos to the tranquility of country living offered a much-needed respite. The lengthy drive to his rural haven usually spared him from being called back in. On the flip side, though, once he got in the ambulance, it was hard to clock out. His coworkers and supervisors knew that once he was gone, he was gone. Today's tally of hours was an exception, an additional three hours beyond his usual shift. The thought of another long day loomed over him like a dark cloud. The miles stretched out before him, each one bringing him closer to home yet highlighting the sheer distance he had yet to cover.

The image of a dry bed emerged in his mind. So drained was he that the prospect of a meal held little allure; candy bars, sodas, and coffee had sustained him throughout the day, but their consumption had also sabotaged his appetite. Thoughts of nourishment could wait at least until the morning, when, hopefully, he would wake up with renewed strength and a better appetite.

As the rural landscape unfolded before him, the constant patter of raindrops on the windshield provided a hypnotic rhythm akin to the lullaby of the night. The rain, both a relentless companion and a soothing background noise, added a layer of introspection to his journey home. Each drop seemed to wash away a bit of the day's stress, allowing him to decompress as he drove further away from the urban sprawl. The world outside his window became a blur of green and grey, a calming contrast to the stark brightness of the hospital's fluorescent lights.

Yet, just as the tranquility of the countryside beckoned, a flash of emergency lights up ahead disrupted the serene ambiance. A car with flashing lights and a raised hood—the universal symbol of car trouble—awaited attention on the roadside. He slowly drove past, with his primary desire being a swift journey home without further delay. The man standing in the rain peered under the hood. The image, momentarily reflected in Brad's rearview mirror, triggered an internal debate. The echoes of his professional oath rang in his mind—the commitment to provide assistance based on human needs with concern, kindness, and respect.

With a resigned sigh, Brad slowed to a stop. Despite the weariness clinging to him, he shifted the gearshift to 'R' and slowly reversed past the stranded vehicle before pulling in behind it. He trudged through the rain to the awaiting driver, extending a helping hand. "Hey, friend. Anything I can do to help?" The drenched man, with glistening silver and black hair welcomed the unexpected assistance. His weary eyes met Brad's with a mix of relief and gratitude, the universal human connection forged in moments of distress.

"Yes. Do you know anything about cars? Because I sure don't."

"That depends. What's it doing?"

"At the moment? Nothing. I was hoping to at least get it home."

"How long have you been out here?"

"About twenty minutes. You're the first to come by, and I thought you weren't going to stop."

"I thought about driving by. I'm just getting off from a long shift at work. Can I give you a ride somewhere or call someone for you?"

"I guess this would make a good commercial on the importance of having a cell phone, huh? Could you call my son? He's at work, but I have his number on his card I keep in my pocket."

Brad entered the code to unlock his phone and looked up. "Okay. What's the number?"

Before he could dial, the perfectly round hole of a gun barrel stared back at him, abruptly halting the sequence of events. "Wait! Don't shoo—"

# 11 | ELEVEN

Except for the subtle hum of the elevator, the ascent from the basement to the third floor was uneventful. The state-of-the-art police building, a futuristic marvel in design, offered a stark contrast to the archaic speed of its elevators. The relentless journey between floors felt like an eternity, a stark reminder that technology, even in the most advanced settings, can still lag behind expectations.

In the respite between floors, Zeke, ever the intuitive detective, delved into the labyrinth of questions echoing in his mind. Motivation and the twisted thought process of the killer became the focal points of his mental exploration. *Was the perpetrator born a killer, or did circumstances mold them into one? What is their occupation? Have they claimed lives before, or is this a chilling debut? Why are they killing people?* Zeke's mind raced through the possibilities, dissecting each thought with the precision of a surgeon. The anticipation gnawed at him, each unanswered question a thorn in his side.

The threshold to serial killer territory was a grim realization, requiring at least three separate murders in quick succession. Though mass murderers and spree killers fell under this classification, Zeke clung to the hope that they weren't dealing with a serial killer. Yet, a lingering doubt gnawed at him, and he speculated that a third victim might surface sooner rather than later. His thoughts cascaded into a classification exercise, employing Holme's Typology to categorize the killer as either act-focused or process-focused. He mentally sifted through the evidence, trying to draw a line between the lack of clues and the methodical mind of a murderer.

Act-focused killers struck swiftly, while process-focused ones reveled in the slow agony of their victims. Memories of Isaac and Isaiah, the summer twins seeking retribution for their tormented past, lingered in Zeke's mind as an example of process-focused killers. Struggling with the shooter's classification, he leaned towards act-focused due to the quick kills, though the true nature of the killer remained elusive. His mind flitted back to the crime scenes, replaying the details, searching for a pattern that might reveal more about the perpetrator's psyche. Each piece of evidence, every nuance of the crime scenes, became a puzzle piece in the larger picture he was trying to assemble.

On the opposite end, Myrna's analytical mind fixated on the tangible aspects of the case—gender, age, and the enigma of potential multiple killers. The distinct bullets and handguns used in each murder puzzled her. In the absence of concrete evidence, she was left to navigate a sea of speculation and assumptions. Her thoughts drifted to the profiles of known killers, comparing and contrasting them with the scant evidence at hand. She considered the possibility of a mastermind who meticulously planned every detail versus a more impulsive, disorganized killer.

Myrna contemplated the proximity of the killer to the victims, pondering whether the lack of suspicion might hint at a woman, who typically appeared less threatening. The possibility of the killer being part of a trusting profession, perhaps a police officer or firefighter, took root in her considerations. She visualized each potential scenario, weighing the likelihood of each hypothesis and sifting through her mental database of criminal profiles. The process was painstaking and exhaustive, but Myrna knew that any detail, no matter how small, could be the key to solving the case.

The elevator, a temporary haven for their divergent thoughts, finally reached the third floor. The doors parted to unveil a bustling scene—an open floor adorned with uniformed officers, desks, and the din of ringing phones. It could be mistaken for a call center if not for the badges and uniforms that distinguished it. The organized chaos of the police station was a sharp contrast to the quiet contemplation of the elevator ride.

Navigating through the activity, the detectives exchanged pleasantries with officers working with handcuffed perpetrators. Their journey culminated at a glass door adorned with gold-and-black letters proclaiming 'Chief Peter Bostwick.' The chief, visible through open mini blinds, welcomed them with a wave. His office, a blend of order and disarray, reflected the dual nature of his role as both leader and fellow investigator.

Seated in front of the Chief's worn wooden desk, Zeke and Myrna embarked on the task of updating him on the case. Chief Bostwick, with a mix of toughness and compassion, listened intently as Myrna outlined the puzzling details—two murders, different bullets, and handguns. His weathered face remained impassive, though his eyes betrayed the concern he felt for the growing complexity of the case. The room's atmosphere was heavy with unspoken questions and the weight of responsibility.

Zeke chimed in. "We are investigating professions that would not raise suspicion of being out during the thunderstorm. We think people in these professions would not be seen as a threat, which would allow them to get close to the victims."

"We're currently looking into tow truck companies, specifically 24-hour ones at the moment," added Myrna. "We both agree that police officers would not raise suspicion or be seen as a threat to someone in need, but we would need your permission to add them to our list of possible professions to investigate."

"So, you think that the murderer could possibly be a police officer?" probed the chief.

"Yes, sir," replied Myrna.

"Let's focus on these other professions first. If we exhaust these efforts, then I may allow a 'quiet' look into patrol officers. Looking into our own carries a heavy possibility of fallout that we go far beyond this case. It takes years to build trust, but it can be lost in the blink of an eye. If word got out about it and it's not a patrolman, the trust in the precinct would be gone." The weight of his experience lent gravity to his advice, and both detectives nodded in agreement, recognizing the wisdom in his words. "Understood," said Zeke.

As they exited the Chief's office, Myrna's phone rang, and a revelation hung in the air. The sound cut through the ambient noise of the station, drawing Zeke's attention immediately.

"Don't tell me," said Zeke, his voice heavy with premonition.

She ended the call, her expression grave. "And then there were three."

The weight of her words hung between all of them, a grim confirmation of Zeke's earlier fears. They exchanged a look of mutual understanding, knowing that things had just gone from bad to worse.

# 12 | TWELVE

The latest victim's lifeless body laid beneath a drenched crime scene sheet. This spot marked the spot where fate took a dark turn. Myrna, seasoned in the grim rituals of her profession, conducted a meticulous examination, weaving slow, deliberate laps around the tragic scene. The rain, heavy and unyielding, poured down in torrents. With a practiced gesture, she pulled back the sheet, unveiling the victim's face—the telltale round hole in his forehead, surrounded by clumps of damp, blackened blood. The scene was a macabre tableau of violence and mystery, the latest chapter in a story that was growing darker by the day.

"Extra pictures of this, please," Myrna requested from the CSU photographer, her focus shifting to the victim's abandoned phone. She scooped it up and shook off the excess water before securing it in a plastic bag. The prospect of finding fingerprints felt like a long shot. "Maybe we'll get lucky with a phone number or something," she mused, her thoughts hinting at a desperate hope. The phone, waterlogged and battered, seemed to hold the last secrets of a life cut short.

A few feet away, tire tracks etched in the mud revealed the presence of another vehicle. Zeke, ever vigilant, surveyed the surroundings. "No disabled car this time, no driver in distress," he observed, prompting a call to a nearby officer to turn off the idling truck. The sudden silence accentuated the gravity of the scene as Zeke joined Myrna at the victim's side. "Anything?" he inquired, his voice low and measured, reflecting the seriousness of the situation.

"Not much," Myrna responded, drawing his attention to the water-filled tire grooves. "There was another car here. There's also a cell phone."

Zeke dropped a revelation that added a chilling layer to the unfolding narrative. "Did you know that our victim was an off-duty EMT?"

"What?" Myrna's surprise mirrored the shock of the discovery.

"Yep. Name's Bradley Kowalski."

The possibility that he was the killer, caught in a twisted reversal of roles, loomed in their thoughts. Myrna took a long, deep breath and exhaled. "You think he was a victim or an unlucky suspect?"

"I thought about that," admitted Zeke, his analytical mind probing deeper. "But there are some things wrong with the picture."

Myrna pressed for details; her curiosity piqued. "Like?"

"Well, in the previous murders, victims were targeted in their disabled cars—a stark contrast to this scenario. And if our EMT was the killer, where's his gun? Wouldn't it be somewhere near his body?" Zeke questioned.

The detectives exchanged a moment of silent contemplation; each lost in their own thoughts about the implications of this new development.

"If the shooter was a potential victim, then wouldn't they have stayed and called the police to share what happened?" continued Zeke, his mind working through the possibilities.

"What are you thinking?" asked Myrna, her eyes narrowing as she tried to read his thoughts.

"I think we are dealing with the same killer who decided to change his tactic," Zeke proposed, steering the investigation in a new direction.

"How so?" Myrna's curiosity deepened, her mind racing to keep up with Zeke's logic.

"I think that instead of looking for disabled cars, he pretended to be in need of help this time," Zeke explained, pointing to Kowalski's still-running truck. "Our EMT must've stopped, got out to see if he could help—"

"—and lost his life for being a good Samaritan. I guess that explains the phone. Maybe he was trying to call for help for the driver," Myrna completed the thought.

"Yeah," Zeke agreed. "I think our killer baited him. Not him specifically, mind you. It could've been anyone. It just so happened that our EMT here is accustomed to helping people."

"…and they took advantage of his good heart," added Myrna. "Then they left him on the side of the road in the pouring rain like some kind of animal. Damn bastard."

"Yep," replied Zeke.

The revelation shifted their perspective, unveiling a new layer of calculated menace. Myrna pondered, "So now he's luring his victims instead of hunting them?"

"It looks that way. Or maybe they are using both tactics," Zeke replied, his mind working through the implications.

"Shit. If that's the case, then that means he intentionally selected this location."

"It's definitely off the beaten path," Zeke agreed, his eyes scanned the remote surroundings.

A moment of thoughtful silence enveloped them. Myrna proposed a closer examination, leading Zeke to the victim's body and unveiled another unsettling detail. "Look at the size of the gunshot wound. It's larger than the ones on the other two."

"Way larger," Zeke agreed, his eyes narrowed as he examined the wound more closely.

"What if we're dealing with multiple killers? It would explain the change in M.O.," Myrna speculated, her mind racing with the possibilities.

"Yeah. But it could also mean a single killer attempting to create confusion," Zeke countered. "I say we work it from both angles until one of them hits a dead end."

"Agreed. Given our current situation, do you think we should continue looking into towing companies?" Myrna sought his opinion, her mind already considering the next steps.

Zeke took a deep breath as he grappled with the expanding web of possibilities. "Good question. I'm not sure about the answer, though." He paused again, considering the complexities of the case. "Okay, I have one more for you."

"What's that?" Myrna's attention focused, eager to hear his thoughts.

"Have you noticed that all three of our murders occurred on rainy days? I mean, there were plenty of dry days in between, but no one died on them in this manner."

"Oh, hell," Myrna exclaimed. "How do we warn people about not accepting any help on the road—or providing any—without creating panic about a possible psychopath fascinated with killing people in the rain?"

"I hope I'm wrong," Zeke admitted, "but I think we may need to start watching the weather forecast. This IS the rainy season."

# 13 | THIRTEEN

The ceaseless, high-pitched whining reverberated through the air of the dimly lit room. Akin to the disturbing hum of a dentist's drill, it was an unsettling sound that grated on the nerves. The acrid scent of burning metal permeated the atmosphere.

At the heart of the lone table stood a plexiglass-encased marvel — the Ghost Gunner, a CNC milling machine with the uncanny ability to craft firearms devoid of serial numbers. It operated as a secretive artisan of weapons, shrouded in the shadows of illegality, ingenuity and lawlessness. The attached laptop, armed with Computer-Aided Design (CAD) drafting software, conducted a symphony of precision. It orchestrated the intricate dance of a cobalt drill bit as it etched away at the metal, birthing yet another untraceable firearm. The machine hummed with calculated and deliberate movements.

The solitary observer, seated in a lone chair, divided his attention between the mesmerizing machine and a flat-panel television mounted on the wall. The glow from the screen casted a ghostly pallor over his face, highlighting the lines of weariness and resolve etched into his features. The abrupt silence that followed the completion of the machine's task was fleeting, soon replaced by a soft hum as it retracted its bits, readying itself for the next mission. The observer's eyes flickered with a mix of satisfaction and anticipation; the silence amplified the pounding of his heart.

Normally, his wife would have descended to check on him by now, her footsteps a familiar intrusion into his secret world. However, today was different – an unusual respite from the incessant nagging about missed promotions, financial struggles, and the haunting echoes of a troubled past. The absence of her voice, a constant harangue of discontent, provided an unexpected solace. His thoughts drifted to the painful memories etched into his psyche, starting with a stepfather who constantly belittled him, predicting a future of insignificance. The memories replayed like a broken record, each word a dagger that had left lasting scars.

Tony Kendall once had aspirations of climbing the corporate ladder within the power company. For years, he toiled away in the heart of the electrical infrastructure, learning the intricate workings of substations and power distribution systems. He was a man driven by a desire to prove himself, to rise above the low expectations set by those around him. However, despite his dedication and technical prowess, he found himself overlooked and overshadowed by colleagues who seemed to effortlessly ascend the professional hierarchy. The bitterness of each missed opportunity gnawed at him, a constant reminder of his perceived inadequacy.

Tony's simmering resentment reached a boiling point when he discovered that he had been passed over for promotion once again. The final straw came when a younger, less experienced colleague leapfrogged him in the race for career advancement. This perceived injustice became the catalyst for a malevolent transformation that would soon grip the city in fear. His anger, once a smoldering ember, now burned with an intensity that demanded action. Long dead from the slow decay of alcoholism, his stepfather's taunts lingered like persistent shadows, a cruel reminder of a life burdened by self-doubt. His wife, too, met an untimely demise, not from alcohol but from a mid-sentence bullet through her forehead. Surprisingly, he didn't feel a thing. The act, so sudden and final, had left him numb.

His mind, momentarily distracted, snaps back to reality with the beep from the CNC machine. Meticulously inspecting the newly forged weapon, the man donned lighted magnifying glasses, scrutinizing it for imperfections. His work was a display of methodical precision, a testament to a life and career where carelessness was an unaffordable luxury. The weapon, sleek and deadly, gleamed under the harsh light, each curve and edge a testament to his skill and determination.

With the finesse of a seasoned artist, he retrieved a box of bullets, selecting from an arsenal ranging from 9MM to 357 Magnum. The 357, a powerhouse among handguns, became the chosen companion for this creation. A box of 357 ammunition and a small bottle of oil joined the assembly line on the table. His movements were deliberate, each action performed with the confidence of a man who knew his craft intimately. His gaze fixed on the television while he lubricated the chrome-colored handgun and wiped off excess oil. His fingers danced with the bullets, each finding its place in the magazine. Satisfied with his meticulous choreography, he locked the loaded magazine into the pistol grip and inserted yellow foam plugs into his ears.

Moving to a black metal box in the corner, the man tilted it forward, revealing a tapered spout resembling a funnel. This unassuming contraption was his firing range – a compact clearing box. With calculated precision, he loaded the gun and pulled the trigger, and the room was engulfed in muffled pops and flashes of light. The sound, concealed by the box, ensured his neighbors remained oblivious to these dark rehearsals. An empty metallic click signaled the end of the performance. Coughing from the lingering gunpowder, he leaned back, his weapon cooling beside him. His attention shifted to the television just as the local weatherwoman took the screen.

------------------------------

"Good evening, folks. We are in for another few days of heavy rain in response to a weather system moving in from the north. We have the chance of rain at 100%. Don't be startled by the rumbles of thunder and flashes of lightning we expect to accompany the storm. Keep your umbrellas and rain jackets handy, but if you don't have to be outside, don't. This is Susan Gary for Channel Nine News."

------------------------------------

Tony nodded approvingly at the forecast. He was aware that using his truck again would be pushing his luck. The rain, a convenient cover – and ally - ensured fewer witnesses and easier escapes. He contemplated a different strategy, like the recent use of his car, to evade detection as he plotted his next move.

# 14 | FOURTEEN

Myrna and Zeke found themselves ensconced in their cramped, slightly claustrophobic office, a space originally designed for solitary work but adapted by them for their collaborative efforts. The room was dominated by the formidable 'twins'—two identical, worn-out gray metal desks that invoked memories of a 1970s grade school classroom.

The room, designed for a lone detective, felt even "cozier" with the addition of a portable whiteboard, a vital tool for their investigative endeavors. Despite its snug confines, Myrna and Zeke had managed to create a functional workspace, occasionally joking about Zeke's size in their hovel, even jesting about the potential lethality of breaking wind in their confined quarters.

On this particular occasion, Zeke meticulously reviewed his spiral notebook, a repository of hastily scribbled notes, while Myrna prepared with dry-erase markers in hand. They then commenced their intricate dance around the whiteboard. Squeaks from the markers echoed intermittently as they crafted timelines, mapped out locations, and delved into the specifics of each murder.

The trio of victims—Sarah Jessup, Arnold Mallard, and Bradley Kowalski—had met their demise under varied circumstances. Sarah was killed during a storm on the southwest border of Dallas; Arnold met his end during heavy rain on the eastern border; and Bradley's life was extinguished in the western rural part of the city during another rainstorm.

Zeke pondered aloud, "You think there's a connection with the locations?"

Myrna considered the question, "I thought so at first, but other than the Kowalski murder, the location was based on chance."

Their dialogue seamlessly shifted between analysis and speculation. "I wonder if he—or they—have completely changed their tactic, or will they go back and forth between the two methods?" Zeke mused.

"Or will they use an entirely new one?" Myrna added, her mind contemplating the elusive patterns of the killer or killers.

Transitioning to the subject of leads, the detectives faced the challenge of creating pathways in the absence of tangible clues. Single killer versus multiple killers, the towing company theory—all were angles that demanded exploration. The Chief's rejection of the rogue cop idea left them with the towing companies as their primary focus.

Their gaze then shifted to the realm of evidence, where every detail, no matter how subtle, held significance. In the absence of a murder weapon and fingerprints, they scrutinized the positioning of the bodies and the direction of travel of the vehicles. The meticulous nature of the crimes suggested a careful, methodical killer adept at manipulating situations to their advantage.

Stepping back from the whiteboard, the detectives examined their investigative tableau. Heads turned in a slow-motion synchrony, akin to watching a tennis match. A buzz from Zeke's phone broke their concentration, redirecting their attention to the unfolding developments.

Placing the cap on his marker, Zeke turned to Myrna with a serious expression. "I think you'll want to see this."

"See what?" Myrna inquired.

Zeke extended his phone towards her, revealing a weather update. "Yep, we got another heavy rain system heading our way. It looks like we only have a day or so before it hits."

Myrna's reaction was immediate. "We gotta hurry. Let's figure out how many towing companies we're dealing with. I'll check Dallas if you'll check surrounding cities."

Seated at their desks, they clacked away at their keyboards. Moments later, Zeke shared his findings. "I checked the companies within a twenty-mile radius of the city limits. I got hits on Garland, Plano, and Arlington."

Myrna, jotting down notes, responded, "I got nineteen within Dallas city limits. Eleven of them are twenty-four-hour companies. I say we divvy up the twenty-four-hour ones here first before heading to the other cities. If we go together, we may run out of time before the next weather system."

"Okay," Zeke agreed. "I'll take the ones in the North and East of town, and you can check out the others."

Myrna, contemplating the potential challenges of obtaining a warrant, voiced her concern. "I'm not sure how far we'll get without a warrant, and it's a long shot to get one."

"Yeah. Our only probable cause is our theory," Zeke acknowledged.

"That means we need to use other tactics to get what we need out of them."

"Time to go old school."

With their plan in place, the detectives prepared for the arduous task ahead. The sense of urgency was palpable, driven by the looming weather system that seemed to coincide with the killer's timeline. Each step they took, every piece of information they gathered, brought them closer to unmasking the person or persons behind the murders. The whiteboard, now filled with notes and connections, served as a visual representation of their progress and the complexity of the case.

As they geared up to visit the towing companies, they knew they were racing against time and an unpredictable adversary. The rain, once a mere background to their investigation, had become a critical factor in their strategy. It wasn't just about solving the case; it was about preventing another murder during the storm.

# 15 | FIFTEEN

Amidst the light but persistent rain, the stocky man navigated the congested streets of downtown Dallas in his aging blue sedan. Traffic was slower than usual due to the annual governmental meeting at the Dallas Convention Center, a gathering of politicians, aspirants, corporate representatives, and media personalities. For him, it was more of a nuisance than anything else, disrupting the city's flow and monopolizing law enforcement resources.

Oddly, he found solace in the increased police presence, seeing it as a diversion for them, allowing him to adapt his dispatching methods without the constant scrutiny. Reflecting on his original strategy of feigning vehicle issues, he acknowledged its limitations. Luck played a significant role, but how many times could he expect that to work?

Driving away from the bustling city center, he headed towards the suburban outskirts, hoping for another opportune moment to satisfy his unsettling desires. His impatience grew as minutes passed without a police car in sight. Perhaps people were avoiding the rain, or word about his activities was spreading. How could it not?

Needing a moment to gather his thoughts, he turned left towards the park, a serene retreat for contemplation. Nestled on the east side of town amid thick trees, the 400-acre park offers a variety of spaces, but he preferred the secluded back, away from children and sports enthusiasts.

As he ventured deeper into the park, he arrived at his favorite spot—
a large man-made pond encircled by a quarter-mile track. A geyser
adorned the pond's center, and a covered gazebo on a wooden pier
provided a peaceful retreat. The park layout unfolded around him,
revealing a fenced-in dog park, open fields, and a gravel running trail
through the woods.

Surprisingly, a few people were present, engaging in activities like
running and exercising despite the rain. "*What the hell is wrong with people?
Are they really that obsessed with being fit?*" he thought to himself, perplexed
by their dedication to fitness. He observed a man entering the running
trail. Without hesitation, he repositioned his car and moved towards the
trail's other end, intending to conceal himself within the woods.

Powerwalking into the trees, he positioned himself to strike while
remaining within a quick escape radius. Out of breath and covered in
rain and sweat, he waited, contemplating how to make the runner stop.
Just as the runner's footsteps approached, he realized his shooting skills
were subpar, necessitating close proximity for a precise shot. With
limited time and creativity, he devised an impromptu plan. The runner
reached the top of the incline to find a man on his knees, leaning against
a tree, clutching his chest. Concerned, he asked, "Hey. You okay?"

Leaning into his act, the man pleaded for help, drawing the runner
closer. "My…chest… I think I'm having…a…" Before he could finish
his sentence, he fell to the ground. "Please…help me…"

The runner hustled over and knelt beside him. "Oh my God. Are you okay? What can I do?"

"My pills…"

"You have pills? Where are they?"

The distressed man pointed toward his left side. "…my…pocket."

The runner rummaged through all the pockets on the man's left side. He checked the raincoat pocket. Nothing. He patted down the thigh and pressed his hand into the man's pants pocket.

Distracted and under duress, the runner never saw the man retrieve the handgun from the right pocket of his yellow rain jacket. It's too late.

In a moment of sheer terror, the large handgun bucked in response to the heavy caliber round exiting its barrel, ending the runner's life instantly.

The shooter rose, silver and black hair clinging to his face like a wet mop. Blood droplets adorned his impassive expression as he surveyed the lifeless body of the felled, good Samaritan runner. A cautious scan for witnesses revealed none, prompting him to locate the lone expended shell casing. To his dismay, it's nowhere to be found.

His internal alarm clock signaled the need for a swift exit. With determination, he trudged away, leaving behind the lifeless body of the unsuspecting runner and the steady patter of rain echoing through the hauntingly quiet woods.

He drove away from the park with his mind racing through the events that just transpired. The thrill of the hunt and the kill, the adrenaline rush that followed, and the chilling satisfaction of seeing the life drain from another human being.

The stocky man drove aimlessly for a while, his thoughts a mixture of satisfaction and anticipation. The rain continued to pour, a relentless reminder of the cleansing ritual he had just performed. His mind wandered to the next time, the next victim, the next thrill. He knew he must be careful, that the police presence might increase, and that his methods might need to change. But for now, he reveled in the memory of his latest kill.

Pulling into a quiet suburban street, he parked his car and took a moment to compose himself. The rain had let up slightly, but the streets were still slick and reflective. He checked his appearance in the rearview mirror, noticing the speckled traces of blood dotting his face. Satisfied, he stepped out of the car and walked toward his home, blending seamlessly into the neighborhood's tranquility.

Inside, he removed his wet clothes and took a long, hot shower. The water cascaded over his body, washing away the physical traces of his crime, but the memories remained vivid in his mind. He stepped out of the shower, dried off, and dressed in comfortable clothes. The man headed to his living room, where he poured himself a drink and sat down to watch the evening news.

The television broadcasted images of the ongoing governmental meeting, the increased police presence, and the weather forecast predicting more rain. He smirked, knowing that the rain was both a blessing and a curse for his dark activities. He took a sip of his drink and leaned back, his mind already plotting the next move.

As the rain continued to fall outside, the man felt a sense of peace. The world around him remained oblivious to the monster in their midst, and for now, he was content. But deep down, he knew that the urge to kill would return, stronger and more demanding than before. And when it does, he would be ready.

# 16 | SIXTEEN

Raindrops splattered against the windshield of Myrna's police-issued cruiser, creating a mesmerizing dance on the glass. The dark gray and black sky above signaled the arrival of the storm predicted days ago. Parked in the lot of a popular local truck stop, she patiently waited for Zeke. Their meeting was crucial, a discussion about the next steps in their investigation into the roadside murders that had yielded frustratingly little progress so far.

In the preceding days, the detectives tirelessly canvassed 24-hour towing companies within Dallas city limits, hoping to unearth any link to the unsettling series of murders. However, their efforts bore no fruit, leaving them empty-handed once again. Time, always a critical factor in police work, had become even more pressing with an imminent thunderstorm threatening to unleash its fury. The prospect of another murder hung in the balance only heightened the urgency.

As Myrna sat in thoughtful silence, the parking lot transformed into a watery expanse. Passing vehicles navigated through the rising water, and the towering 18-wheelers made a beeline for the fuel pumps, seeking refuge from the impending tempest. Some drivers, resigned to the inevitability of the storm, prepared to wait it out, while others, more optimistic or perhaps desperate, forged ahead, hoping to outrun the weather.

Feeling the weight of the investigation bearing down on her, she rubbed her temples, succumbing to the beginnings of a headache. She retrieved a large bottle of pain relievers from the glove compartment, a makeshift remedy for the stress-induced discomfort. Downing three pills with a sip of water, she considered their next move.

Zeke's arrival was heralded by an intensification of the storm. He jumped out of his car and into Myrna's, the relentless rain soaking him during the brief transition. Before he settled into the seat, Myrna cut straight to the chase, "Any luck on your end?"

Busy wiping his face, Zeke responded with a defeated tone, "Nope. You?"

"Nothing."

The question of their next steps lingered in the air. Myrna hesitated, torn between checking the remaining towing companies in the city and expanding their search to 24-hour companies in neighboring cities. The storm, however, altered her perspective.

"This storm's got me thinking differently," she admitted.

Zeke, curious, probes further, "How so?"

"I say we focus on keeping anyone else from dying during this storm. Then we can check out the other companies afterward."

Acknowledging the challenge, Zeke pointed out, "We're going to need help."

"I know. I'm going to see if the Chief can provide some extra patrols. At least until this storm moves out."

"That might be tough, considering we have the statewide government meeting tomorrow."

"I guess we'll take what we can get."

Myrna retrieved her phone, intending to call the Chief. However, before she dialed, a utility truck passed by, sending a wave of water onto her cruiser. Undeterred, she watched as the truck parked, prompting Zeke to inquire about her gaze.

"Remember our conversation about workers in the storm?" Myrna asked, pointing towards the utility truck.

Zeke followed her gaze. "Yeah. We were wondering which ones wouldn't look out of place outside of tow truck drivers. Why?"

She pointed again, "What about them?"

Examining the utility workers, Zeke realized, "I'll be damned. Electric company workers wouldn't look out of place, especially with outages and downed lines. That means we need to add them to our already long list. I wonder how many electric companies there are?"

Refocusing on her phone, Myrna decided, "I'll call the Chief to see if he can provide extra patrols, at least through the storm, with special attention on utility workers, tow trucks, and disabled vehicles."

The storm raged on outside, but within the confines of the police cruiser, a plan began to take shape, fueled by the detectives' determination to unravel the mystery despite the impending tempest.

Myrna dialed the Chief's number, her voice steady despite the chaos outside. "Chief, it's Myrna. We need some additional patrols focused on utility workers and tow trucks during this storm. Can we get some extra hands on deck?"

Zeke listened intently as Myrna negotiated with the Chief, his mind already racing through the logistics of their new plan. They had to act fast, knowing that each passing moment brought them closer to another potential crime scene.

The Chief agreed to allocate additional resources, albeit reluctantly, due to the impending governmental meeting. "Thanks, chief." She hung up with a sense of relief washing over her. They had a temporary solution in place, but the real challenge lay ahead - stopping the killer before he struck again.

Turning to Zeke, Myrna updated him on the Chief's response. "We're getting some help. Now, let's focus on narrowing down our list of utility companies and figuring out where to start."

Zeke nodded, his expression determined. "I'll reach out to Tyler to see what he can get us on utility companies along with recent utility company activities or incidents." While Zeke made his call, Myrna leaned back in her seat, the tension in her head easing slightly.

# 17 | SEVENTEEN

A formidable set of metal double doors welcomed the detectives into the precinct's ground floor hall, setting the tone for the technological prowess that lay beyond. The black, flashing door access control system, mounted on the right wall, emitted a rhythmic red LED light, while the opposing silver intercom box, complete with a camera lens, stood ready for communication. The modern, almost futuristic setup was a stark reminder of the high-tech operations that kept the precinct running smoothly.

Zeke, accustomed to navigating both the physical and technological realms, looked into the camera lens and reached for the silver button engraved with 'CALL.' However, before his finger could make contact, a voice resonated from the intercom box, "Hey, Zeke. C'mon in."

With a confirming "buzz" and a subtle click, the door granted them entry, and Zeke strode through, Myrna close on his heels. The temperature shift within the room always caught Zeke off guard, irritating his hot-naturedness. The culprit? An array of computers, servers, and mysterious devices that defy identification. Myrna, seemingly immune to the discomfort, found amusement in Zeke's irritation.

"Dang. It's hot as hell in here," Zeke remarked, wiping a bead of sweat from his forehead.

Myrna chuckled, her amusement evident. "It's not that hot. Oh, I forgot. You're always in a constant state of your own personal summer."

Amidst the banter, Tyler Stevens, the Technology Director of the Dallas Police Department, emerged from a back office. Navigating the maze of desks and cutting-edge technology, he approached, extending a hand to Zeke. The warmth in the room was momentarily overshadowed by the icy acknowledgment he offered to Myrna.

"Tyler. My man," Zeke greeted, engulfing Tyler's hand in a hearty handshake.

"Hey, Zeke," followed up with a bone-dry "Myrna," the tension palpable. Their history of strained interactions was well known, with Myrna's impatience and social disconnect casting a shadow over their professional rapport.

Undeterred by the chilly reception, Zeke and Tyler exchanged pleasantries, much to Myrna's dismay. She viewed small talk as an unnecessary diversion, but Zeke, a believer in the power of relationships, understood the importance of rapport and kindness. Myrna's resistance to this lesson was a persistent challenge rooted in her own complex history and her mother's influence. Tyler, sensing the need to steer the conversation toward business, inquires, "So, what can I help with?"

"We need information on electric companies in the area," Zeke replied, cutting to the chase.

Tyler, feigning nonchalance, quips, "That's it? I thought you were going to give me something hard this time. Oh, well, beggars can't be choosy, huh?"

Myrna interjected with a pragmatic tone, "I'll keep that in mind for next time. Just remember that if we're in here to see you, it's already tough enough for us."

"So, I get to be the Oracle to your Batman," Tyler suggested.

"Something like that, but you do know that Oracle's a woman, right?" Zeke countered a hint of amusement in his voice.

"Of course, but she's also an autodidact, just like me. If I'm Oracle, who is Myrna?" Tyler mused, his tone light but probing.

Myrna, largely ignored, brooded in response. Zeke, aiming to ease the tension, inquired about the new addition to Tyler's family, prompting a brief respite from the professional exchange.

"She's finally sleeping through the night, thank God. But still as beautiful and amazing as ever," Tyler responded warmly, the mention of his daughter softening his demeanor.

"Time for another one, then," Zeke teased, his tone playful.

Tyler peered over his glasses with tiny blue eyes and retorted, "Not a chance, dude. What're you trying to do to me? Look around. I already have hundreds of children here."

Guiding them to a large plexiglass board at the back of the room, Tyler explained the geography of electric companies in Dallas. Zeke and Myrna followed, the dynamic between them ever-present. Tyler's explanation prompted Myrna to question the significance of starting with larger utility companies, provoking a momentarily icy glare from Tyler.

"Sorry," she conceded, and Tyler continued, revealing the presence of GPS-equipped vehicles among the larger utility companies.

Zeke suggested, "Now, let's hope they will share the information with us."

"I'm not sure how much it will help," Tyler admitted, "but I can give you the names of each of the IT Directors, and I'll ask them to help you all they can. Without getting fired, of course."

"Of course," Zeke acknowledged. "This is awesome, Tyler. As always, I appreciate you, man."

With newfound information and a potential plan in place, Myrna and Zeke made their way back through the technologically advanced room to the metal double doors. As the door began to close, Myrna reopened it, poking her head in.

"Thanks, Tyler," she said, her tone sincere.

"Um, you're welcome?" Tyler responded, puzzled by the unexpected acknowledgment. The door slowly closed, leaving a lingering sense of both professional collaboration and unresolved tension in the air.

The detectives stepped out into the cool night air, the rain still falling steadily. Myrna adjusted her jacket, pulling it tighter around herself. "Well, that was... interesting," she remarked, her voice betraying a mix of amusement and irritation.

Zeke nodded, a thoughtful expression on his face. "Yeah, but we got what we needed. Let's head back to the office and see what we can piece together with this new info."

# 18 | EIGHTEEN

The relentless downpour persisted over Dallas, wearing on Myrna's patience as she yearned for an end to the incessant rainy season. Zeke, however, remained undeterred, adapting to the punches nature threw their way. While the heavy rain threatened to hinder the detectives' progress, their resolve remained unbroken, determined not to let the weather impede their investigation.

In Zeke's sleek, metallic black car, the constant veil of water cloaked them from view. Occasional flashes of lightning briefly illuminated the car. They patiently waited for a brief respite in the downpour, aiming to make a swift exit from the car to the building without succumbing to the rain's relentless assault.

Their destination is the Dynamic Energy Corporation, the first of several electric companies in the area that they planned to visit. The hunch that the killer may be connected to a utility company led them here. Although it might seem like a stretch, they're running out of viable leads and places to investigate. Opting to check with larger companies first, Zeke and Myrna hoped to leverage the GPS installed in their vehicles for potential insights.

Seizing a moment of reduced rainfall, they dashed to the building's edge beneath a long brick awning. Shaking off excess water, they contemplated their chances of finding crucial information in this seemingly unlikely place.

"Let's hope we have better luck at finding something that will help us here," Myrna commented.

Zeke nodded in agreement.

With no warrant in hand, just speculation, a dearth of leads, and an increasing sense of desperation, the detectives pressed on. Their saving grace was the Chief granting them extra patrols during the storm, a temporary relief until the statewide governmental meeting tomorrow. The lack of a warrant forced them to rely on their cunning to extract information from their chosen targets.

Satisfied with their level of dryness, they entered the building, only to be greeted by an expansive lobby that more closely resembled an upscale hotel than an electric company. A young woman behind a colossal front desk, accompanied by an overweight, armed security guard, awaited their approach.

Identifying themselves as Detectives Sontiago and LaPorte, Myrna requested to speak with the information security officer, Mr. West. Despite lacking an appointment, Myrna made it clear that conducting investigations rarely adhered to scheduling norms.

The discomfort of the young receptionist, Emily, became apparent as she checked Mr. West's availability. Soon after, they were granted access, and Mr. West descended from the chrome elevator to meet them.

After the initial exchange, Myrna and Zeke delved into the purpose of their visit, explaining the investigation into vehicle damage potentially caused by a utility truck. They lied. Mr. West expressed surprise at the allegation, emphasizing the prominent logos on their vehicles and the unlikeliness of confusing their trucks with another.

The detectives informed him that they were checking with all electric companies with blue trucks. The conversation turned to the utility company's GPS data, but Mr. West hesitated. "I think I need to consult our legal department before sharing such information."

Undeterred, Myrna reassured him, "We were hoping to save some time from having to get a warrant issued, but oh well. We'll be in touch."

Back outside, under the protective awning, they prepared for a mad dash to their vehicle. Just as they were about to brave the rain, a faint call caught their attention.

"Detectives. Detectives."

Turning towards the source, they spotted a man in a plaid shirt running towards them. They turned in unison in the direction of the call. A moment later, the small-statured man stopped just short of them. Out of breath, he tried to speak.

"Detectives…Tyler…got something…"

Zeke placed a hand on the man's shoulder. "Easy, dude. Take your time."

After gaining his composure and with a little more control, he began again. "My name is Dakota. I'm a friend of Tyler."

"Okay. What about Tyler?" asked Zeke.

"Tyler texted me a little bit ago and said that two of his detective friends may be stopping by in need of some technical information. He asked if I would do him a favor without getting fired. It took me a while, but I downloaded some information that may be of help to you."

Dakota pulled out a black flash drive from his pocket. It has no markings sans the gray, inscribed '128GB' on its side.

"What's on it?" asked Myrna.

Dakota informed them the encrypted data on the flash drive held the movements of the company's utility trucks over the last three months, particularly those with drivers who turned the GPS off and on.

"Wait a minute," said Myrna. "The drivers can turn off the GPS?"

"Yeah," replied Dakota. "Isn't that stupid? I mean, why install it if it can be turned off? Anyway, Tyler has the key to decrypt and extract the information."

Zeke accepted the flash drive and Dakota's condition: they must forget where they got it.

As Dakota hurried back to the building, Zeke reflected on the unexpected camaraderie Tyler seemed to feel towards them. He playfully nudged Myrna, remarking on the effectiveness of friendliness in gaining cooperation.

"Did you notice that Tyler referred to both of us as friends? Imagine that. More flies with honey, Myrna, more flies with honey. You will learn soon enough, Catwoman."

With a chuckle, Zeke sprinted towards the car, leaving Myrna to ponder the nuances of interpersonal dynamics amidst the relentless rain.

# 19 | NINETEEN

The atmosphere in the precinct's elevator area hung heavy with anticipation as Myrna and Zeke waited for one of the four elevators to ferry them to the ground floor. Myrna, a bundle of nerves and impatience, paced in a tight circle, alternating between facing the pairs of opposing elevator doors. She glanced at her watch repeatedly, pressing the call button in a rapid succession. Her frustration was evident as she muttered about the elevators being slower than usual. Zeke, on the other hand, turned the flash drive over in his bear-sized hand, contemplating its potential significance.

After what seemed like an eternity, an electronic chime broke the silence. Myrna swiftly turned in search of the elevator, and their chariot arrived—the third elevator. Myrna charged toward it, eager to board, but the doors were yet to open. A few muffled, adjusting clunks later, the doors revealed an empty cabin. Myrna entered promptly, pressing the glowing amber 'G' button before Zeke could join her. The elevator descended in silence, carrying them to the ground floor of the precinct.

As the elevator doors parted, the familiar sight of the I.T. department with its metal double doors and flashing access control system greeted them. Zeke took the lead as they exited the elevator, and he pressed the air call button on the audio-visual security system mounted on the wall.

The magnetic thunk resonated, signaling their entry. Moving swiftly, they headed straight to Tyler's office, nestled in the rear corner. He greeted them with enthusiasm. "Detectives. What can I do you for?"

Zeke presented the flash drive to him, a crucial piece in the puzzle they hope will crack the case. "You can do this for us," Zeke stated, his tone reflecting the urgency of the situation.

Tyler, ever the inquisitive tech expert, queried, "What's that?" as he shot a look at Myrna, who offered a simple explanation. However, Tyler's glance at Myrna implied more than just curiosity.

Zeke proceeded to explain the events at the electric company and how Dakota, an unexpected ally, provided them with the encrypted drive. Tyler, pleasantly surprised by Dakota's involvement, took the flash drive to a non-networked laptop to check it for viruses. Satisfied, he took it to his laptop, and lines of code scrolled rapidly across the screen.

Zeke peered over Tyler's shoulder and asked, "Are those lines good news?" Tyler responded without taking his eyes off the screen. "It's too early to tell," he replied. "I need to extract and decipher the data to determine its usefulness."

Myrna checked her watch. The hum of computers filled the air. Zeke, in an attempt to ease the tension, struck up a conversation with her about family, particularly her elusive mother.

"I wish I could tell you," said Myrna.

"What do you mean?" asked Zeke.

"I mean that I have no clue where she is or what she's doing. I only hear from her when something is wrong, or she needs something. I swear the woman hates me."

"I know you don't believe that," replied Zeke.

"Then why is it that she never tells me she loves me? How hard is it for her to show me appreciation or even consideration? It's as if I haven't accomplished anything in my life. She's never acknowledged anything I've done or mentioned the words 'I'm proud of you.' I've racked my brain and can't for the life of me figure out what I did wrong other than being born."

Zeke continued to listen. He could feel his partner's frustration, anger, and, most of all, hurt. She had never been the same since her father's death. It was probably the last time she felt loved. Especially since, according to Myrna, her mother had never been very affectionate. He chose his next words carefully, knowing that his partner rarely showed her vulnerabilities.

"Those are all good questions," he replied. "The only one with the answers to them is your mother. Have you ever asked her these questions?"

"No."

"Why not?"

"I don't know."

"Sure, you do. You just may not be ready to answer it. Question: When's the last time you told your mom you loved her?"

Myrna shifted her gaze to the floor and raked her fingers through her hair. "It's been a while."

"I know you may not want to hear this, but you may have to be the one to take the first step."

Myrna reflected on her strained relationship with her mother. Her phone rang, disrupting the moment. She recognized the number and answered with reluctance, already assuming it was another ploy for money. However, the call took an unexpected turn.

The initial irritation on Myrna's face gave way to genuine concern. "What do you mean you're in the hospital?" Myrna doesn't buy it. She suspected it was just one of her mother's latest ploys to get some money.

"Appendix? What's wrong with your appendix?" she asked.

Zeke listened as Myrna exchanged words with her mother. Her emotions shifted from frustration to worry.

"Okay. I'm on my way. Tell them I'm on my way."

Myrna shared the news that her mother was at Dallas Memorial, and her appendix was inflamed. "At least I know where she is now," quipped

Myrna. "She originally went to the emergency room for stomach pains," she explained. "I asked her why she didn't call me."

"What'd she say?" asked Zeke.

With moistened eyes, Myrna replied, "She said I would think that she was only calling for money and that I wouldn't care."

Zeke placed a comforting hand on her shoulder. "You and I both know that you do."

'I'm going to run over to the hospital and check on her. Keep me updated?"

Zeke nodded in understanding, offering support. "Call me if you need me," he said as Myrna disappeared through the metal double doors, leaving Zeke alone in the I.T. department, waiting for the outcome of the flash drive analysis.

# 20 | TWENTY

With Myrna occupied at the hospital and Tyler engrossed in decrypting the flash drive's data, Zeke decided to grant himself a mental reprieve. The relentless pursuit of the case had taken a toll on his mind, which continued to churn through leads and clues even during moments of supposed rest. The need for a break was palpable. The yearning for a few moments of respite from the whirlwind of thoughts was upon him.

Parking his sleek black Camaro in front of a bakery-cafe-style restaurant, he aimed for solitude during the quiet period between lunch and dinner. The lunch crowd had dissipated, and the dinner crowd was yet to descend upon the establishment. Seeking the farthest booth from the floor-to-ceiling windows, doors, and the popular open area, Zeke claimed his sanctuary. He settled into the seat, pulled out his journal, and took out an ink pen, ready to put his thoughts on paper.

As soon as he prepared to jot down the date, the ambiance of the restaurant shifted. A few patrons filtered in, occupying the booth catty-corner to him. The lunchtime hustle transitioned into a quieter atmosphere as people engaged in homework, consultations, or writing. The restaurant became a haven for those seeking a moment of solitude or productivity.

Despite the external stimuli, Zeke's journal page remained stubbornly blank. He had been journaling since childhood, a coping mechanism recommended by his therapist after his father's murder. It had evolved into a tool that helped him balance the overload of data, memories, and emotions in his head and aligned perfectly with the philosophy of Stoicism. Journaling, in a way, acted as his own version of Batman's Alfred, helping him maintain clarity in the midst of chaos.

Pressing the pen to the blank page, he finally wrote the date, attempting to immerse himself in the therapeutic act. However, a distant call interrupted his solitude. "Zeke."

Ignoring the initial call, he continued to write, but the voice persisted. "Zeke."

Looking up, he locked eyes with Dominick, accompanied by his parents. A mix of inconvenience and surprise flashed across Zeke's face. *"Really? You've got to be kidding me,"* he thought.

Before he could complete the thought, the trio stood at his table. "Where have you been, Zeke?" Dominick greeted him with enthusiasm.

Suppressing his inconvenience, Zeke responded, "Hey, Dominick. How ya doing?" He noticed Dominick's unbuttoned plaid shirt, revealing a freshly ironed T-shirt underneath, a stark contrast to their first meeting two years ago.

---

Two years ago, Dominick narrowly escaped becoming the next victim of twin serial killers Isaac and Isaiah. Zeke and Myrna, acting on a faint scream, rescued Dominick from a basement torture chamber. The ordeal left Zeke with physical scars from a gunshot and Myrna with lingering guilt. Dominick, though physically unharmed, beared non-physical scars that have yet to heal fully.

---

"What are you doing here?" Dominick inquired, his curiosity evident.

"Take it easy, Dominick," his parents intervened. "Hi, Detective."

Zeke wore a smile, concealing any inconvenience. "I'm doing well. Just finished eating some lunch." It's a white lie, a façade to maintain a semblance of normalcy.

"That's nice," Mrs. Thomas responded. "We're picking up a to-go order."

"Yeah," Dominick chimed in. "It's movie night. We're gonna watch a movie when we get home. Wanna come?"

Dominick and his parents expressed their gratitude to Zeke after the rescue, evolving their relationship into an unofficial mentorship and big brother to their only child. Zeke, contemplating the mysteries of life, pondered whether he, with his demons, could effectively mentor a teenager and serve as a big brother. He noticed that Dominick was around the same age as he was when his dad was taken from him in a senseless and cowardly act of violence. At fourteen, Zeke lost a role model and hero, whereas Dominick, in his eyes, had gained an extra one.

He had replayed his dad walking from the corner store with a few groceries for his wife and only son, wondering what he must've been thinking. His dad was at the wrong place at the wrong time when a group of hoodlums drove by and began shooting at another group. His dad was cut down in the crossfire. He often wonders how his life would have been different had his dad been around. Would he even be a police officer? Probably not, considering that his death provided the impetus to become one.

Declining Dominick's movie invitation due to precinct duties, Zeke noticed Dominick's disappointment. "Maybe we can get in another game of bowling soon, though. I'm overdue for putting the beatdown on a certain someone."

Dominick grinned. "You talking about me? I let you win the last time."

Zeke pulled out his phone and read the message on the screen.

"Duty calls, huh?" Mr. Thomas remarked.

"Yes, sir. And unfortunately, it calls often."

Mrs. Thomas' square buzzer interrupted, signaling their to-go order. "That's us," she declared.

"See ya, Zeke," Dominick bode farewell, giving Zeke a fist bump before disappearing around the corner with his parents.

Zeke lingered in the booth, disappointed that his writing time was interrupted. While he had found joy in mentoring Dominick, he acknowledged that he could use a mentor himself. He could use a lot of things at the moment. A father figure was on top of the list. You could also add a best friend to the list. A therapist also couldn't hurt.

The restaurant's ambient noises became background hums as Zeke contemplated the complexities of his life and the persistent echoes of his past.

# 21 | TWENTYONE

Myrna's disdain for hospitals was etched in her recent memories—each visit marking a chapter of worry and familial concern. Her journey through the antiseptic-scented corridors had become a familiar odyssey of emotions, and now, she reluctantly stepped through the sliding glass doors of yet another emergency room. The awning overhead bared the bold red letters spelling out "EMERGENCY," a stark reminder of the critical situations that brought people to this place.

The reception area, adorned with plastic chairs arranged in a seemingly haphazard manner, held only a sparse population of occupants. Despite the subtle discomfort of the sterile air, Myrna wondered about the wisdom of clustering those seeking medical aid so closely, especially given the prevalence of various ailments.

She navigated the sea of chairs, making a direct path to the check-in desk stationed almost in defiance of the entrance. Behind the desk, a young man and woman in matching light-green scrubs seemed engrossed in their duties. Myrna was met with a warm smile from the woman before she even voiced her question.

"May I help you, Detective?" the woman inquired, her recognition spurred by the visible badge and gun on Myrna's person.

"Um, hi," Myrna responded. "My mother came in earlier for a ruptured appendix."

"That would be Mrs. Cortés, correct?"

"Correct."

Myrna's internal disapproval surfaced momentarily as she reflected on her mother retaining her maiden name. Her thoughts, however, are momentarily set aside as the receptionist endeavored to locate information about her mother's current status.

"Let me see if I can find out where she is at the moment."

"Okay. Thank you."

While feigning patience, Myrna took in the surroundings—the sterile gloss of the floor, the commonplace sight of a clipboard and pen combo, and the imposing beige doors lining the adjacent hallways. An unsettling chorus of coughs from an emergency room patron behind her amplified her urgency to minimize her time in the contagion-laden environment.

Before Myrna could inquire about her mother, a side door bursts open, unveiling the arrival of a gurney carrying an elderly man shrouded in blankets. The receptionist sprang into action, badge swiped, orchestrating the smooth passage of the medical entourage. The door protectors rattled in protest as the gurney navigated through, and with the same grace, the receptionist returned to her swivel chair as if such incidents were routine.

Finally, with a few clicks on the keyboard, the receptionist announced, "Found her."

"Where?" Myrna queried anxiously.

"She is out of surgery and just arrived in the recovery room."

"May I go see her?"

"Sorry. You will have to wait for them to bring her out. But she has already been assigned to a room. One of the medical staff will take her there once they clear her."

"What's the number?"

"339. You can go up and wait for her there. Elevators are on the left side of the hall to your right."

"Thank you."

"You're welcome. I hope your mother has a speedy recovery."

Myrna managed a half-hearted smile. "Yeah. Me, too." She turned toward the elevators; a mixture of apprehension and hope colored her thoughts, blending into the complex tapestry of emotions that hospital visits often entail.

The hospital's familiar labyrinth of hallways beckoned as she headed toward the elevator bank. She paused briefly, contemplating the efficiency of the medical staff navigating these corridors daily, each one a microcosm of life and death. The scent of disinfectant lingered in the air, a reminder of the constant battle against infection within these walls.

Entering the elevator, she pressed the button for the third floor. The doors slid shut with a muted whoosh, cocooning her in the quiet solitude of the moving box. Her mind replayed the scenes from earlier: the urgency of the medical team, the controlled chaos of the emergency room, and the reassuring demeanor of the receptionist.

# 22 | TWENTYTWO

Myrna's ascent to the third floor via the elevator was swift, and as she emerged, the labyrinth of hallways stretched before her. She followed the signs, and the journey to room 339 was accompanied by the symphony of medical equipment, a dissonant melody that became more pronounced as she advanced. The sporadic beeps and tones, the lifeblood of the hospital's soundscape, echoed through the corridor.

The hallways were bustling with activity – a dynamic tapestry woven by the presence of computer carts stationed like sentinels, nurses engaged in meticulous data entry, and the constant movement of medical staff weaving in and out of rooms. The central nurse's station stood as a focal point, a bustling hub orchestrating the seamless rhythm of patient care. Myrna, amidst this orchestrated chaos, couldn't help but wish for a similar command center in her investigative pursuits, something to monitor all aspects of the case in real-time. Alas, wishful thinking remained a whimsical desire in her world.

Room 339, nestled at the corner formed by intersecting halls, beckoned Myrna forward. Upon entering, she was met with the stark minimalism of the space – two beds with corresponding carts, a flat-panel television mounted on the wall, and an array of medical paraphernalia. The room's ambiance, laden with oxygen tubes, tanks, and electronic devices, painted a vivid picture of the gravity of the situation at hand.

It had been a while since Myrna found herself in the clinical embrace of a hospital room. The last instance was after her father's heart attack, a somber memory that offers no solace. Zeke's recovery room had seen her presence, but it was far from a warm homecoming. Now, surrounded by the sterile environment, she was keenly aware of the absence of something more profound – the warmth of her mother's love. However, her thoughts gravitated towards the negative aspects of their relationship, a well-worn path marked by anger and resentfulness. Myrna realized that this absence had played a pivotal role in shaping her into a person with a resilient yet guarded outlook on life. Despite this awareness, she found herself standing at the precipice of change, unsure whether she possessed the strength or desire to mend this fractured connection.

As she waited for her mother to arrive, memories of her father – the unconditional love he offered – flooded back, creating a poignant undercurrent. The hospital room, with its clinical precision, became a canvas where past and present intermingle, and Myrna grappled with the complexities of her emotions, bounded by the ties of family and a desire for something more.

Outside, the hallway buzzed with a muted intensity. Voices drifted through the closed door, snippets of conversations between healthcare providers and patients' families. Myrna listened attentively, catching fragments of reassurance and concern, a reminder of the interconnectedness that defined the hospital's ecosystem.

In the quiet lull between medical updates, she retreated into introspection. She recalled moments of tenderness shared with her mother amidst the turbulent currents of their relationship. Yet, the scars of past disagreements lingered, etched into the fabric of their bond like invisible ink waiting to be revealed.

The minutes stretched into an hour, then two, as Myrna wrestled with impatience and hope. She scanned the room, taking note of every detail—the sterile sheets, the faint scent of antiseptic, the distant hum of activity beyond the walls. These surroundings, once foreign and unwelcome, now enveloped her in a cocoon of familiarity.

Finally, the door swung open, heralding the arrival of a nurse clad in scrubs. Myrna's heart skipped a beat as she met the nurse's gaze, searching for clues in the subtle shift of expression. Relief flooded her senses as the nurse offered a reassuring smile.

"She's doing well," the nurse assured, her voice a balm to Myrna's frayed nerves. "They're just finishing up some final checks, and then you can see her."

Myrna nodded, gratitude swelling within her. She sunk into a chair by the window, allowing the weight of uncertainty to lift from her shoulders. Outside, the sun casted a golden glow over the hospital grounds, a reminder of the resilience that resided within every patient and caregiver.

# 23 | TWENTYTHREE

Zeke's journey to Spindletop Power Company was marked by the rhythmic hum of the city, the urban pulse that propelled him toward the dispatch supervisor's office. The anticipation lingered in the air as he approached the building, wondering if this visit would yield the breakthrough they desperately needed. The city around him bustled with life. The skyscrapers rose like sentinels, watching over his quest for answers.

Upon reaching the dispatch supervisor's office, Zeke was met with an atmosphere buzzing with the orchestrated chaos of radio chatter and administrative duties. The office was a hive of activity, with employees moving purposefully, telephones ringing, and the hum of conversation creating a symphony of efficiency. The dispatch supervisor, a seasoned individual with an air of authority, greeted him with a firm handshake, ready to assist with any inquiries.

"Good afternoon, Detective. What brings you here today?" the supervisor inquired, his eyes reflecting a hint of curiosity. His demeanor is professional, yet there's a warmth that suggested a willingness to help.

Zeke got straight to the point, expressing the need for information regarding the GPS systems on the company's vehicles. The initial revelation is disheartening – like the other electric company - drivers could manually toggle the GPS on and off. "They can turn it off? Why have it then?" inquired Zeke. A momentary dip in hope washed over Zeke, but the supervisor's next revelation turned the tide.

"However," the supervisor continued, leaning slightly forward as if to share a secret, "what our drivers might not know is that we've installed tracking chips in all our vehicles. The system runs in the background, unnoticed by the drivers themselves. We've got a wealth of data that could be of help to you."

A spark of renewed optimism ignited within Zeke as he realized that their quest for information wasn't in vain. The company, albeit unwittingly, had provided the detectives with a valuable resource. The supervisor pledged cooperation, willing to share the data, though acknowledging the need for the detectives to sift through the information. His eyes conveyed a sense of partnership, an unspoken agreement to aid in the pursuit of justice.

Zeke, now armed with a potential breakthrough in the case, departed. The city's pulse seemed louder now, each step carrying him forward with purpose. The skyscrapers casted long shadows as he navigated the streets, his mind racing with the possibilities unveiled during his meeting.

Back at the precinct, Zeke reflected on the collaborative effort ahead. The data from Spindletop Power Company held promise, a digital breadcrumb trail that could lead them closer to uncovering the truth. At least, that was his hope. He still had to follow multiple leads, including the tow truck companies.

Back at his desk, he pulled out his notepad, jotting down key details from the meeting. The supervisor's assurances echoed in his mind, a reminder of the teamwork driving their investigation forward. Each piece of information, no matter how small, had the potential to tip the scales in their favor.

Hours passed as Zeke immersed himself in analysis, the hum of the city outside fading into background noise. The glow of his computer screen illuminated his determined expression—a detective on the brink of unraveling a mystery that had consumed their attention for weeks. He pored over the data, cross-referencing vehicle movements with known crime scenes, searching for patterns that might reveal the killer's identity.

As night descended over the city, Zeke leaned back in his chair, weary yet buoyed by a sense of progress. Tomorrow would bring new challenges, but for now, he savored the satisfaction of a day well spent— a step closer, he hoped, to bringing closure to those affected by the killer. Whoever they were.

# 24 | TWENTYFOUR

Myrna re-entered her mother's room, a small stack of magazines clutched in her hand; the crinkling sound of glossy pages interrupted the sterile ambiance. She had just returned from making a quick purchase from the hospital gift shop. Her mother had been in a state of semi-consciousness, still under the lingering effects of the anesthesia, when she was wheeled into her hospital room. Myrna wondered if she even noticed her absence during the short excursion. The room, with its muted colors and faint smell of antiseptic, felt cold and unwelcoming, amplifying Myrna's sense of unease.

Armed with a stack of periodicals, Myrna hovered near the bedside, torn between the desire to elicit a smile from her mother and the haunting realization that she knew so little about the woman who brought her into the world. She wondered about her mother's interests, hobbies, or any form of entertainment that might provide a fleeting escape from the monotony of hospital life. The magazines felt like a small but meaningful gesture, an attempt to connect on some level, to bridge the emotional gap that had always existed between them.

As she flipped through the magazines, the glossy covers reflected her uncertainty. A subtle mix of genres graced the stack – from fashion and travel to home decor and health. Myrna's choices, a mosaic of interests, were an attempt to bridge the generational gap and offer solace to her mother. The weight of not truly knowing her mother's tastes lingered in the silence that enveloped the room.

Presenting the magazines with a tentative smile, Myrna hoped they would be a source of distraction, a small comfort in a trying time. However, an unexpected clash ensued as her mother's reaction diverged from the anticipated appreciation. "I don't read any of these," she said, her voice weak but clear. "Why did you get these?" she continued, her eyes narrowing in confusion.

"I, I, I wasn't sure what you liked, so I got different ones," replied Myrna, her voice faltering. The room, once poised for a touch of joy, now held the residue of tension. Myrna, caught off guard by this unexpected discord, decided to give her mother space, her heart heavy with the unspoken complexities that underlined their relationship. The disappointment in her mother's eyes stung more than she anticipated, a reminder of their strained bond.

"I have to go, mom. Call me if you need me," she said softly, her words a mix of retreat and confusion.

As the door swung shut behind her, Myrna took a moment in the quiet hallway to process the conflicting emotions. The hospital's ambient hum served as a backdrop to her contemplation, echoing the intricacies of familial bonds and the uncharted territory of understanding the one person who should be known the best. Stepping away from the room and too caught up in her own emotions, she missed the whisper from her mother's lips saying, "I need you." The faint plea, unheard, hung in the air like a ghost.

In the corridor, Myrna paused to collect herself as the fluorescent lights casted stark shadows on the linoleum floor. Her thoughts swirled with regret and longing, grappling with the distance between them despite their physical proximity. She replayed the scene in her mind, searching for clues in her mother's expression, trying to decipher the unspoken words that hung heavy in the air. The realization that she might have misinterpreted her mother's needs added another layer to her guilt.

The hospital hallway stretched before her, a corridor of uncertainty and unresolved questions. Myrna's footsteps echoed softly as she walked, each step a measured pause in the ongoing narrative of their relationship. The memories of their few shared moments flickered in her mind, a collection of fragmented interactions that painted a picture of a relationship in need of healing.

Myrna's mind drifted to her childhood, moments when her mother seemed distant, lost in her own world. She remembered trying to get her attention, seeking her approval, and often feeling like she was grasping at something elusive.

Determined not to let the moment slip away, Myrna decided to return to her mother's room. She knew that their relationship wouldn't be mended with a single gesture, but it was a start. As she approached the door, she took a deep breath, ready to face the emotional complexity that awaited inside. The possibility of reconciliation, of understanding, of truly seeing each other was worth the effort.

Stepping back into the room, Myrna saw her mother looking out the window, a pensive expression on her face. She walked over and placed the magazines on the bedside table. With her voice filled with sincerity, she asked, "What kind of magazines would you like?"

# 25 | TWENTYFIVE

The detectives arrived at the park for the latest crime scene, yet another shooting. The persistent wind carried the scent of rain that lingered in the air. At the moment, there was no connection to the previous murders, three of which occurred on the roadside. Although two of the victims were found in their car, the other was left lying on the side of the road. The only facts that connected them were that they were all shot at close range and on the roadside. But that is where the similarities ended. They were all different ages and from different occupations and walks of life. One victim was female, and the other two were male. Even the caliber of the bullet was different for each of them. The other similarity between the murders and the bane of frustration was that there was absolutely no evidence to be found.

As the rain began to drizzle, Myrna felt a subtle relief that, at least for now, this murder didn't seem connected to the first two. Seeking respite from the relentless pace of the previous cases, she secretly yearned for a breakthrough. Realistically, she knew they needed a lead, a thread to unravel the mystery. Hopefully she would have better luck with this case.

Zeke scanned the periphery of the crime scene, squinting against the wind-driven rain, while Myrna, undeterred by the elements, crossed under the yellow tape to take a look at the body.

With the wind tugging at her coat, she squatted down, pulled the sheet back, and was met with a disturbing sight - a large hole dead center in the jogger's forehead surrounded by what looked like a sprinkling of black pepper. A closer look revealed the telltale signs of gunpowder embedded in the skin, emphasizing the close-range shot.

The rain intensified. Myrna, now battling the elements alongside the investigation, muttered a solemn "*Whoa*" under her breath, confronted by the reality of not just another shooting but the eerie possibility that this one may be connected with the others.

The wind-driven rain played a relentless percussion on her detective's jacket as she continued her examination. Dark streaks, likely blood, traced a macabre path across the victim's face, resembling running mascara. The crimson trails ran from the hole over the glabella, down the nose, across the lips, and finally, down to the chin. It was a morbid painting of brutality, starkly contrasted against the gray backdrop of the storm. Even the rain, attempting to wash away the horror, only added to the eerie ambiance.

In typical running gear, the victim was frozen in the act of fitness — shorts, a tank top, no-show socks, and running shoes. Myrna, despite her seasoned experience, shivered, her soaked clothing clinging uncomfortably to her. Still squatted, she replaced the sheet and rubbed the lower part of her jaw, a ritual born out of the unease that settled in her gut. It's not the sight of death that disturbed her, but the unsettling pattern — another victim, shot in the head from close range, just like the others.

Standing up, she felt the weight of the rain-soaked wind against her, but her detective's mind was already in motion. Four victims, all with a bullet to the forehead at close range. The realization hit her like a punch. "Shit."

Amid the relentless elements, Zeke's booming voice broke through the buzzing of the crime scene. "Myrna," he calls, "I think you'll want to see this." She scanned the surroundings and spotted a waving Zeke just beyond the crime scene tape. She looked around to see which direction she should go.

Carefully stepping over the lifeless body, Myrna navigated through the rain-soaked terrain toward Zeke. "What's up?" she inquired, her words almost drowned out by the persistent drumming of raindrops on her detective's shield.

Zeke doesn't speak but instead pointed, directing her attention to the rain-soaked ground. Nestled inconspicuously in a small cluster of brush at the base of a tree lies one…lone…shell casing.

Squinting against the wind-driven rain, Myrna asked, "Is that what I think it is?"

Without shifting his gaze, Zeke confirmed, "Yep."

"You think it's from this shooting?"

"I don't know of any other reason for it to be here," replied Zeke, his words partially swallowed by the sound of raindrops assaulting the foliage around them.

"Talk about a lucky break," said Myrna.

"At this point, it's better to be lucky than good."

As the rain continued to pelt them, Myrna shared her concern about the uncanny similarities between the murder of the jogger and the two roadside victims. She emphasized the different caliber of bullets used in the first two cases and speculated that, if connected, this one likely involved a different caliber as well. A ripple of hope echoed in her voice, yearning for an end to the grim pattern. She hoped like hell that she was wrong.

Zeke broke the somber moment. "You're probably not wrong."

"Why'd you have to say that?" asked Myrna.

"Because," said Zeke, "If you're thinking what I'm thinking, and we are dealing with one killer..."

Myrna interrupted. "Or killers."

"Or killers," quipped Zeke, "then that means that the killer has changed their M.O. Again."

"I think that's exactly what it means," said Myrna.

Many mistakenly think that serial killers are motivated by sexual compulsion. They also think that mass murderers strike out in anger. But they don't often hear about the blend of them. And that is the angry killer. The one who strikes on separate and unrelated occasions to convey frustration, exert control or deliver payback.

"Worse still," said Zeke, is that this killer is cold, calculating, unfeeling, and angry as hell. Yet he didn't overkill his victims. He seems to have a controlled rage. The question is: What are they so angry about?"

"Good question," replied Myrna. For now, I guess we need to visit ballistics so they can tell us that the casing is from anything other than bullets used on the other victims."

"Yep," said Zeke, "who knows, maybe there's a fingerprint or at least a match of the cartridge in IBIS." IBIS is the Integrated Ballistic Identification System.

"Now THAT would be nice," said Myrna. "I'll meet you there."

Undeterred by the persistent wind and rain, the two detectives headed to their respective vehicles.

# 26 | TWENTYSIX

The shell casing from the park was meticulously mounted on a horizontal rod held steady with utmost precision. Positioned in front of a high-powered magnifier and camera combination, it casted an enlarged projection onto a large computer monitor. The split screen displayed the shell casing on the left side, while the right side projected and compared the images of countless shell casings within the vast repository of the Integrated Ballistic Identification System (IBIS). This cutting-edge system served as law enforcement's technological sentinel, capable of comparing both ballistic evidence types found at crime scenes against its expansive inventory of recovered or test-fired projectiles and casings.

Delving into the intricacies of firearms, it was a little-known fact that every firearm bears unique characteristics. The barrel of a weapon imparts distinct markings on a projectile when discharged, and the breech mechanism leaves its own indelible imprint on the cartridge case. These markings, etched by the breech face, firing pin, extractor, and ejector, become vital clues for forensic investigation. The patterns are as unique as fingerprints, providing invaluable leads for solving crimes involving firearms.

In the realm of firearm examination, few can match the prowess of Lishentikka Patel, the DPD's premier firearm examiner. Born into a family of scholars in Mumbai, India, Lishentikka's journey into forensic examination was a path less traveled. From a young age, her fascination with science and meticulous attention to detail set her apart. Following her passion, she pursued a degree in Forensic Science at the University of New Haven. Her academic excellence and dedication to her field were evident from the start, paving the way for her future success.

Her expertise in forensic ballistics emerged early in her career. A chance encounter with a seasoned firearms examiner sparked her interest in the intricate world of ballistic identification. Her relentless pursuit of knowledge led her to the United States, where she joined the Dallas Police Department (DPD) as a firearms examiner. She immersed herself in the study of firearms and ballistics, quickly establishing herself as an authority in the field.

Over the years, Lishentikka became the linchpin of the DPD's forensic team, earning a reputation as a scrupulous and insightful examiner. Her proficiency in handling cutting-edge technologies, particularly the Integrated Ballistic Identification System (IBIS), elevated her status to the premier firearm examiner and an invaluable asset not only to the department but at the state and federal levels as well. Her contributions to high-profile cases brought her recognition and respect from her peers.

Tasked with scrutinizing the shell casing presented by the detectives, she embarked on a laborious and time-consuming process. The severe stress and eye strain overshadowed her work, but the use of cutting-edge technology still outpaced the antiquated examination techniques of bygone eras. Recognizing the potential benefits, the ATF and the Department of Treasury birthed the Information Superhighway known as IBIS, creating a formidable tool for law enforcement in solving firearms-related violent crimes.

The Automated Firearms Ballistics Technology facilitated the rapid and automatic comparison of crime scene bullets or cartridge casing evidence with other images in its database. However, the system doesn't conclusively identify matches — that nuanced task falls to a skilled firearms examiner. Instead, the technology produces a shortlist of candidates, assigning a numerical probability of a match for each, thereby eliminating the need for the examiner to visually sift through unlikely possibilities. This amalgamation of high-level analysis and visual scrutiny expedites the elimination of non-matches, optimizing the time spent on comparisons. The precision and efficiency of the system are crucial in the fast-paced environment of forensic investigation.

Despite countless hours invested in examining, comparing, and searching for matches, Lishentikka finds herself at an impasse. The absence of a match raised several potential scenarios. It could imply that the shell casing was related to the crime scene but had not been entered into the database or that the firearm used in the jogger's murder had not been previously employed in other criminal activities. Regardless of the conclusion, the stark reality remained unaltered — the casing held no answers for Myrna and Zeke. With a sense of deflation, Lishentikka picked up the phone and dialed the detectives to convey the less-than-stellar news.

Listening to the dial tone, she reflected on the frustrating nature of her work. For all the successes and breakthroughs, there were just as many dead ends and unanswered questions. Her mind raced through the possibilities, wondering what could have been missed or if another piece of evidence would eventually lead them to the truth. She understood fully that persistence and dedication didn't always pay off.

On the other end, Myrna answered the call, her voice tinged with anticipation. Lishentikka delivered the disappointing news with a heavy heart, detailing the exhaustive efforts made and the current lack of leads. Myrna's silence on the other end spokes volumes, the weight of the case pressing down on them both.

"I'm sorry, Detective," Lishentikka said softly, her voice filled with genuine regret. "We'll keep looking, and if anything comes up, you'll be the first to know."

"Thanks, Lishentikka. We appreciate all your hard work," Myrna replied, her tone resigned but appreciative.

Lishentikka ended the call, took a deep breath, and returned to her station. Despite the setback, she remained resolute. In her lab, surrounded by the tools of her trade, she refocused on her work, knowing that the next piece of evidence, the next clue, might hold the key.

# 27 | TWENTYSEVEN

Tyler eased back in his chair, the weariness etched on his face evident from the dark circles under his eyes. The mammoth, wall-mounted computer monitor loomed over him like a digital behemoth, showcasing a mesmerizing cascade of intricate code. To the untrained eye, it may resemble an unintelligible jumble, but for Tyler, it unfolded like a captivating narrative, a poetic dance of algorithms and commands. The sheer size of the 75-inch display dwarfed the typical living room television.

He diligently sifted through the labyrinth of code, each line a potential clue in the intricate tapestry of the investigation. The focus of his scrutiny lay on uncovering GPS data that could tie Dynamic Energy Corporation's utility trucks to the crime scenes. The absence of information from other electric companies in the area amplified the pressure on Tyler's shoulders. The anticipation of unearthing a breakthrough weighed heavily on him, a feeling only intensified by the silence emanating from the detectives regarding additional leads. The room was filled with the soft hum of servers, a constant reminder of the digital world he navigated so expertly.

Tyler yearned for that elusive moment when the code revealed a hidden truth, cracking the case wide open. His seasoned expertise hungered for the challenge of solving a high-profile murder, a stark contrast to the more straightforward nature of cases involving digital paper trails and technological fingerprints. The combination of location and timing became a puzzle he is determined to solve. The hours slipped by unnoticed as he delved deeper into the data, his mind a whirl of possibilities and potential breakthroughs.

With eyes scanning the scrolling lines, a flicker of recognition sparked within him, and he bolted upright from his chair, momentarily forgetting his fatigue. With measured steps, he approached the colossal monitor, reaching out tentatively as if he could physically touch the lines of code. His fingers traced an intriguing section on the screen, his mind racing to comprehend the significance of the revelation. The code before him started to align with the patterns he's been searching for, each line a piece of a larger, more complex puzzle.

A surge of excitement propelled Tyler into action. He darted back to his desk, snatched the phone from its cradle, and pressed the speed dial, summoning Zeke with an urgency that echoed through the dimly lit workspace. The phone rang in sync with the rapid pounding of Tyler's heart. When Zeke's voice crackled over the line, Tyler could barely contain his enthusiasm. "Zeke, you won't believe this. I think I might have found something. Can you drop by?" His voice was a mix of excitement and relief, the culmination of hours of intense focus.

A palpable pause ensued before Tyler heard Zeke's response. "Okay. See you soon." The phone disconnected leaving Tyler to immerse himself once more in the digital labyrinth as his fingers danced across the keyboard in a feverish symphony of discovery. The revelation reenergized him, the fatigue momentarily forgotten as he dove back into the code.

The minutes ticked by as he continued to analyze the data. He documented his findings meticulously, ensuring every detail was captured for when Zeke arrived. The anticipation of sharing his discovery with the detectives fueled his determination, pushing him to delve even deeper into the data.

# 28 | TWENTYEIGHT

Zeke and Myrna treaded through the labyrinthine corridors of the IT department, following the familiar route to Tyler's office. The walls were lined with server racks humming with data, and the air was filled with the faint scent of electronics. The door swung open at their approach, and Tyler beckoned them inside with a warm, anticipatory grin, his eyes sparkling with excitement.

"Come in, come in," Tyler exclaimed, his excitement unmistakable. The room was a blend of organized chaos, with screens displaying various streams of data and charts. "We came as soon as we could," Zeke replied, eager to dive into the revelations Tyler had in store for them. "What do you have for us?"

"Take a look at this." Tyler motioned towards his imposing wall monitor, where a mosaic of information unfolded. He began elucidating the intricate details, seamlessly shifting between the monitor and his laptop like a frenetic ping-pong ball. The screen displayed maps, GPS data, and timelines, all interwoven into a complex web of information.

Zeke, ever the pragmatist, patiently allowed Tyler to delve into the technicalities before interjecting, "Um, excuse me, Tyler, but may I ask a question?" Tyler responded with a nod, encouraging Zeke to continue. "I was following you for a little bit, but then I lost you when you started using... before you started using some of your, how can I say, technical language."

A knowing nod from Myrna signaled her agreement, acknowledging her own impatience and the strain in her relationship with Tyler due to it. Despite the tension, Zeke reassured Tyler, "It's okay. If you're excited, we're excited."

With newfound clarity, Tyler adjusted his explanation, steering clear of excessive technical jargon. He unveiled his discovery – the connection between the first roadside murder's location and the movements of a Dynamic Energy truck. Animatedly, he shared, "This truck was not only nearby; it was on the same road as the murder. Based on GPS data, it drove right by where you found the car."

The detectives absorbed the revelation, a mix of hope and skepticism lingering in the room. The detailed map on the screen showed the exact route of the truck, marked with timestamps. "It could be nothing, but I thought that this could be more than a coincidence," Tyler cautiously added, sensing the need to manage expectations.

Myrna and Zeke maintained thoughtful silence, prompting Tyler to elaborate further. "But it could be nothing. Besides, the truck wasn't near the other murders. It was parked at the company," he said, pointing to another screen showing the truck's location logs.

Sensing Tyler's diminished enthusiasm, Zeke injected a dose of optimism. "You may be on to something, Tyler. The truck wouldn't be near the other murders since they all had a different M.O. Even if it's nothing, we need to talk with the driver of that utility truck to see what, if anything, they saw that night."

"Yeah. If you can give us more information on the truck, we could go back to Dynamic to find out who was driving it that night," Myrna chimed in, echoing Zeke's sentiment. Her voice carried a note of determination, ready to follow any lead.

Tyler, somewhat deflated, apologized for not having more substantial evidence. "It's better than nothing, and it's definitely more than what we have," Zeke reassured him, grateful for the lead, however faint. His eyes met Tyler's, conveying gratitude and encouragement.

As the detectives turned to leave, Tyler interjected, "Detectives?" Intrigued, they faced him once more. "I think I can save you a trip."

Zeke, curious, inquired, "How so?" His brow furrowed slightly, a hint of intrigue in his gaze.

"I did some digging and learned that the driver of the truck was Tony Kendall. He has been with Dynamic Energy for 28 years. He's married with no children and lives in the Old West District in the Pemberton subdivision in a split-level house. Nothing in his record suggests any criminal activity, but you may be interested to know that he was off work on the day of all the other murders."

Tyler handed Zeke a slip of paper containing Tony's address and phone number. Zeke playfully remarked, "You are really trying to earn that Oracle title, huh?" His smile was broad, a mix of appreciation and amusement.

# 29 | TWENTYNINE

Myrna's eyes narrowed with intensity and purpose as she carefully weighed the potential breakthrough in their investigation. "Tony Kendall could very well be the crucial missing link we've tirelessly sought," she mused aloud, a glimmer of cautious optimism coloring her voice. "Then again, he might just lead us down yet another fruitless path. Nevertheless, at this juncture, any lead, no matter how uncertain, is worth pursuing."

Zeke, renowned for his unwavering skepticism and logical approach, commenced tapping away on the keyboard, the rhythmic click-clack of keys resonating through the room. "True," he acknowledged, his tone reflecting a hint of skepticism. "It does appear to be a significant gamble."

"Perhaps. Let's dig deeper into his background and see what else we can find," Myrna suggested, her unwavering determination propelling their relentless quest for the elusive truth.

"Remember that we still have to keep our momentum with the towing companies," Zeke interjected. "So far, the officers haven't hit any paydirt, but there are still lots of locations left to check."

Zeke, ever methodical and organized, meticulously updated the whiteboard with the newly acquired information. He affixed Tony Kendall's DMV photo under the previously blank category labeled

Persons of Interest, constructing a visual roadmap that detailed their evolving investigation.

After a brief yet contemplative silence, Zeke broke the stillness. "You're not going to like what I've found."

Intrigued, Myrna leaned forward, her curiosity now fully engaged. "Like what?" she inquired eagerly.

"Other than possessing a driver's license, home deeds, a few credit cards, and car insurance, there isn't a single blemish to his name, not even a speeding ticket," Zeke revealed, his disbelief palpable in his voice.

"What about his wife?" Myrna pressed on, considering the potential vulnerability in their otherwise flawless facade.

"I'm already on it," Zeke responded promptly. "She's just as pristine as her husband, with an immaculate record."

Myrna sighed softly, realizing the formidable challenge posed by the Kendall couple's seemingly perfect lives. "Let's take a ride. Maybe Mr. Kendall can answer a few questions, and then we can clear him."

Zeke nodded solemnly, acknowledging the uncertainty that loomed over their investigation. "Or he can move from being a Person of Interest to our prime suspect."

# 30 | THIRTY

"Come in, detectives," greeted Derrick, the Lineman Section Leader at Dynamic Energy Company, with a firm handshake. His office exuded an air of authority, adorned with charts displaying intricate electrical systems and blueprints of power grids.

After a few exchanges of pleasantries, Zeke cut to the chase, informing Derrick of the purpose of their visit. "We're here for a background check on one of your employees, Mr. Tony Kendall."

Derrick raised an eyebrow. "Background check? Is he looking for a new job?"

Myrna quickly clarified, "No, nothing like that. We suspect that someone may have stolen his identity and opened all types of new accounts using his information. We believe that he is the victim of an identity theft cell that we are familiar with.

Derrick's expression shifted to one of sympathy. "Wow, that sucks."

"So far, there isn't too much damage, but we don't want it to get to that point," Myrna explained, emphasizing the urgency of their mission.

"I'm not sure how I can help," Derrick admitted, a puzzled look crossing his face.

"We are trying to figure out what's legit and what's not," Zeke clarified, "so if you can tell us a little about Mr. Kendall, it would be helpful for us to eliminate hits that are more likely to be his versus someone full of crap. Let's start with Mr. Kendall's occupation and how long he has worked here."

"He's been with us longer than I've been here. I think close to 30 years, if I'm correct. In fact, he trained me when I was hired a few years ago," Derrick shared a touch of nostalgia in his voice.

"Does he have any hobbies? Is he a good worker? Does he get along with his coworkers?" Myrna probed further.

"He doesn't talk much and pretty much keeps to himself. I've heard from others that he wasn't always that way but has changed over the last year or so. He's a good worker and really knows his stuff. He holds a lot of master's certifications and has even taught a few classes for us. He likes motorcycles, at least that's what I've heard, and he has apparently restored quite a few of them. Other than that, he shows up for work on time and does good work."

"Has he ever received any disciplinary actions that you are aware of?" Zeke inquired.

"Not during my time here," Derrick affirmed.

Myrna chimed in again, "You mentioned earlier that he has changed over the last year in how he interacts with his coworkers. Any idea why they would say that?"

"According to my boss and a few others, it started a little after I was hired."

Zeke, ever discerning, probed further. "You think it had something to do with you being hired?"

"At first, I thought nothing of it, but I learned later that he was an internal candidate for the position but got passed over. According to others, this wasn't the first time."

Myrna delved into the nuances, "You mentioned all of the master-level certifications and being here for nearly 30 years. Is he not qualified for a promotion?"

"Not sure, but it has something to do with his ability to play well with others. Or lack thereof."

"Got it," said Zeke, jotting down notes. "Is he in today?"

"Yes, but most of his days are in the field."

The detectives decided not to ask for his location to avoid raising suspicions about the true purpose of their visit. "Thank you for your time. We'll try to catch him at home this evening."

"Happy to help. I hope you can help him."

"We're doing all we can," replied Myrna, a determined glint in her eye as they left Derrick's office, ready to unravel the mystery surrounding Tony Kendall.

# 31 | THIRTYONE

Myrna observed Zeke engaged in a conversation through his Bluetooth earpiece. The morning sunlight casted a warm glow on the surroundings of the sprawling parking of Dynamic Energy. Tyler, the tech-savvy ally on the other end of the call, provided updates and crucial information. Myrna, her curiosity piqued, wondered what new piece of the puzzle they'd uncovered.

After a series of affirmative head nods and verbal acknowledgments, Zeke finally disconnected the call. "So," he began, a hint of anticipation in his voice, "Tyler spoke with Dakota, and he pinpointed the utility truck near a small substation on the outskirts of town. He's sending the GPS coordinates to our phones."

Myrna, always analytical, contemplated the information. "You think Kendall is connected with these murders?" she inquired, her gaze fixed on Zeke.

Zeke, his hand absentmindedly rubbing his bald scalp, takes a moment before responding. "Part of me hopes so because if he isn't, we're right back to square one. Again. If it is him, I guess a better question is, what is he doing at the substation? Hopefully, he hasn't found another victim."

The prospect of progress in the investigation hung in the air, mingling with the uncertainty that shrouded the identity of the perpetrator. "Then we'd better hurry," quipped Myrna.

# 32 | THIRTYTWO

Basking in the rare tranquility of solitude, Tony immersed himself in his duties at the diminutive electric substation. He is adorned in the quintessential power line uniform, complete with a hard hat, rubber-insulating gloves, goggles, and sturdy boots. This unassuming structure, though small in stature, held the pulse of an intricate electrical power distribution system. It served as a silent guardian that transformed and regulated the voltage of electricity received from the transmission system. Then, it orchestrated its dispersion into the homes, apartments, businesses, and various entities that depended on this pulsating life force.

In his solitary mission, Tony conducted a symphony of inspections and checks, his every move a well-choreographed dance of expertise. His initial focus gravitated toward the transformers, these mechanical maestros responsible for the graceful ballet of stepping up or stepping down the voltage of electricity. Each examination was executed with a precision that only years of experience can bestow.

The next act in this intricate performance unfolded as Tony scrutinized the switching equipment. Breakers, disconnect switches, and fuses—these guardians of the electrical flow commanded his attention. Their task is no less than a dance with the currents, controlling the ebb and flow of electricity while wielding the power to isolate faulty sections of the grid and uphold the sanctity of the system.

Moving seamlessly through the substation, Tony reached the busbars, silent conductors that facilitated the transfer of electrical power between disparate components. Every connection resonated with the harmony of energy transfer, ensuring a seamless flow through the veins of the substation.

His inspection journey continued with a thorough examination of the sophisticated control and protection systems. These watchful sentinels monitored the heartbeat of the equipment, responding to the slightest aberrations in the electrical symphony. Yet today is different—his usually brisk survey of the control and protection systems lingered, a deviation fueled by an undercurrent of anticipation.

The grounding systems received his scrutiny next, followed by the meticulous evaluation of the monitoring and communication equipment, auxiliary systems, and the fortress-like security measures. Substations, he mused, are fortresses safeguarding against unauthorized access and tampering, fortifications essential to preserving the integrity and reliability of the electrical infrastructure.

However, today bared a different rhythm. An unusual tension emanated from Tony as he carried out his inspection. His thoughts betrayed a sinister intent, a departure from the routine.

Suddenly, a dissonant note pierced the air, shattering the serene hum of solitude that accompanied the electricity coursing through the powerlines. Tony remained unfazed, his gaze unwavering, but the source of disturbance became evident—a portable police scanner, a recent online acquisition, crackled to life inside his truck. A disembodied voice emanated from the device, revealing a destination that sent a chill down Tony's spine—it was his current location. The synchronicity was too conspicuous to dismiss as mere chance. Undeterred by the revelation, Tony proceeded with deliberate intent, completing his tasks with an eerie calm.

# 33 | THIRTYTHREE

The gravel crunched beneath Myrna and Zeke's footsteps as they approached the desolate substation; its silver metal structure loomed against the backdrop of an overcast sky. The fence enclosing it was adorned with yellow and black triangular signs warning of electrocution, a stark reminder of the potential danger within. The air was charged with anticipation as they spied Tony's truck parked nearby.

Zeke, known for his unease around electricity, decided to skirt the edges of the substation, a self-imposed boundary to keep the buzzing currents at bay. The crackling of the high-voltage lines above added to his anxiety. Meanwhile, Myrna confidently strode into the heart of the substation, her voice cutting through the silence, "Mr. Kendall? Are you here, sir? We were wondering if you had a moment to speak with us. The words hung in the air, met only by the distant hum of electrical machinery.

The absence of a response was curious. It sent a shiver down their spines. Tony was nowhere to be found, heightening their suspicions. Their sweep was complete. They met at the back of the substation. What started as a mere potential person of interest had now ascended to the status of a potential suspect. Questions dance in their minds, each one more perplexing than the last.

"Did someone pick him up out here?" asked Myrna. How long has the truck been here? Did he drive it here and leave it?"

Without responding, Zeke dialed Tyler. "Any other Dynamic Energy trucks in the vicinity?" he queried. Unfortunately, the response is a disheartening negative. He disconnected the call.

Perplexed, Zeke shared his bewilderment with Myrna, "This doesn't add up. He arrives at work, picks up his truck, drives out here, and leaves? You think Derrick said something to him?" His voice was laced with frustration and confusion.

Myrna, equally baffled, speculated, "It's strange as hell. What are we overlooking? Did someone else take his truck today? If so, where are they? Did he opt for a different truck? If yes, which one?" A sense of relief washed over them momentarily as Myrna acknowledged, "At least there's no rain for a few more days."

"At this rate," said Zeke, "it doesn't matter. He or whoever it is has changed their M.O. three times already. Maybe the rain doesn't even matter anymore."

"We need to find this guy and figure out what the hell is going on," asserted Myrna.

Zeke nods in agreement, a resolve etched on his face. "Let's make a house call," he suggested, his tone firm and decisive.

Concerned about the abandoned truck, Zeke contemplated, "What about the truck?" Myrna, pragmatic yet considerate, responded, "There's nothing we can do with it. We can call Derrick as a courtesy. It might not be much, but it may be a piece of the puzzle."

# 34 | THIRTYFOUR

Myrna and Zeke approached the quiet street of Tony's neighborhood. Zeke parked the car a short distance from a modest gray split-level house. They both took a moment to steady their nerves before getting out of the car.

They walked up to the house, its façade adorned with a touch of suburban charm. The yard, neatly trimmed with a lush carpet of green grass, exuded a quaint serenity. The house, while not imposing, emanated an air of coziness. The size was just right—a home that felt snug without being cramped and a yard that offered just enough space for a breath of fresh air without overwhelming maintenance. Flower beds lined the walkway, adding splashes of color and life to the otherwise muted exterior. A few garden gnomes stood guard near the front porch, adding a whimsical touch to the picturesque scene.

The doublewide cobblestone driveway greeted them, leading the way to the front of the house. An older car rested on the left side near the closed white garage door. On the right, a vintage single-seat Indian motorcycle captured their attention. Its primer gray exterior suggested it was in the middle of a restoration. The motorcycle was a striking piece of history, with saddlebags flanking both sides of the rear fender, almost enveloping the entire rear wheel. It stood as a testament to the affinity for classic machines, seemingly awaiting a fresh coat of paint to restore its former glory.

Zeke, ever the observant detective, couldn't resist checking the motorcycle's temperature. "It's piping hot. Hasn't been here long at all," he remarked, casting a knowing glance at Myrna.

Following their routine, Zeke embarked on a walk around the house's perimeter, examining the surroundings for any hints or anomalies. He moved carefully, his eyes scanning for anything out of the ordinary. Meanwhile, Myrna headed to the front door. She pressed the button on the doorbell camera, eliciting a musical chime from within. The sound was cheerful, almost out of place, given the gravity of their visit.

After a moment, a male voice crackled through the speaker. "Yes? May I help you?" the voice inquired, sounding both polite and cautious.

"Hi. My name is Detective Sontiago. My partner and I were hoping to speak with Mr. Kendall," Myrna responded, her voice steady and professional.

"Speaking," came the reply, catching Myrna off guard.

"Is it possible to come in and speak with you?" she asked, trying to mask her surprise.

"Sure. I'll buzz you in. Come in straight down the hall and turn left. Open the door and come down the stairs to my basement workshop," the voice directed, the tone calm but distant.

Zeke, now back at the door, noticed a hesitation in Myrna's demeanor. "You okay?" he asked, sensing her unease.

She fibs, "Yeah."

"You sure?" Zeke pressed, his concern evident.

"Maybe," she admitted, her voice tinged with doubt.

"What's up?" Zeke asked, his tone gentle but probing.

"The hair on the back of my neck is standing up. Why didn't he come to the door?" Myrna wonders aloud, her instincts on high alert.

Zeke offered a plausible explanation, "Maybe he's busy. Or maybe he has a bad leg or something."

"He did say he was in his workshop," Myrna acknowledged, trying to calm her nerves.

"There you go," Zeke reassured her, though he felt a similar unease.

With a final heartbeat of uncertainty, Myrna entered the house, stepping down into a sunken living room. To her surprise, the interior was much more expansive than the exterior hinted. The house unfolded before her, revealing a depth and breadth that defied initial expectations. The living room was tastefully decorated, with comfortable furniture arranged around a fireplace. Family photos adorned the walls, giving the space a warm, lived-in feel.

Leading the way down the hall, as instructed, she found Zeke close behind, his towering frame nearly filling the entire height and width of the corridor. The air inside the house was cool, a stark contrast to the warm day outside. They moved quietly, their footsteps muffled by the plush carpet underfoot. Myrna and Zeke reached the final door, ready to descend the stairs into Tony's workshop.

# 35 | THIRTYFIVE

The door was solid, painted white with a brass handle that gleamed in the dim light. Myrna paused for a moment, taking a deep breath to steady herself before turning the handle. She carefully navigated the corner at the bottom of the stairs, entering the makeshift workshop concealed beneath the garage.

The room, dimly lit and surprisingly organized, unfolded before her. A machine in one corner caught her eye, accompanied by a small leather stool on wheels. A wall-mounted television and another mysterious metal object completed the ensemble. The centerpiece, a large plush recliner, is cradling none other than Tony Kendall.

Tony, a figure not matching the physical details on his driver's license, reclined in the plush chair. The detectives were struck by the discrepancy in his appearance—the graying disheveled hair, the added weight—evidence of the toll taken by time and, perhaps, the weight of his dark secrets. However, it was not his altered physicality that seized their attention; rather, it was the gleaming chrome handgun pressed under his chin and, in his other hand, a device that appeared to be a remote control.

"Hello, detectives," Tony greeted them, his voice devoid of any emotion. "Please come in."

There was an unmistakable tension as Myrna and Zeke cautiously extended their hands away from their sidearms. The room, once inviting in its simplicity, now held an air of imminent danger. Tony, seemingly unperturbed, raised an eyebrow.

"You like my gun?" he inquired.

"Sure do," Zeke replied with a wry smile. "What is it? A .44 Magnum or .357?"

"Neither. Those are a little too small for my taste. This is a Desert Eagle .50 caliber, custom-made by me with my ghost gunner," Tony pointed to the CNC machine in the corner. "It's the largest bullet of any magazine-fed pistol."

"It'll get the job done, huh?" Zeke remarked, attempting to maintain a semblance of normalcy.

"You better believe it."

Myrna, with her investigative instincts, noticed the remote control in Tony's hand and probed further. "What's that you're holding in your other hand? Some kind of remote?"

"Something like that. It's more of a trigger."

"A trigger? For what?" Myrna's concern deepened.

"For the explosives in the house."

"Explosives?" Zeke questioned, disbelief etching his features.

"Well, the gun is for me, and the explosives are for you."

"For us? What do you mean 'for us'?" Myrna and Zeke exchanged glances, realizing the gravity of the situation. They made a silent pact not to make any sudden moves, and held their hands out to the side.

"Not necessarily for you. It's for whoever happened to figure it all out. It could've been any other officer or detective, but I guess you two were the ones chosen for the case."

Seeking to de-escalate the situation, Zeke employed a tactic to appeal to Tony's sense of control while also being aware of his anger. "Listen, Tony. I think we're okay with us, but not so much for your neighbors. Would you please allow us the opportunity to clear the surrounding area and neighborhood to avoid innocent bystanders being hurt?"

Tony momentarily relinquished control and nodded his approval. "I'll allow it, but only because that is what I want."

"Understood," Zeke acknowledged. "I'm just going to slowly grab my cell phone and make one call. Is that okay?"

Tony, still in control, gave his consent. Zeke seized the opportunity to make a coded call to the chief, updating him on the situation while keeping Tony in the dark about their true intentions.

The detectives engaged Tony in conversation, attempting to stall and hopefully lull him into a false sense of security. "Why were you doing this?" asked Myrna. "Why now? Why not last year or even before that? Why now?

Enraged, Tony yells at Myrna. "I dedicated nearly 30 years of my life to my profession, to that damned company, yet, no matter how hard I worked, no matter how committed I was, I kept getting passed over."

The bitterness of his resentment lingered in the air. His mind wandered to the numerous times he had watched – and trained his new bosses, even those who started years after him, ascend to higher ranks, leaving him behind in the shadows. The persistent sting of rejection had etched lines of frustration on his face, and his once hopeful eyes now reflect a glimmer of despair.

"But my wife was my catalyst. Her constant nagging about why I wasn't making more money, why I wasn't getting promoted." He doesn't mention it, but that, coupled with the constant ringing of his stepfather's words, served as his breaking point. "Before I realized it, I had shot her in the face. The funny thing is that I didn't feel anything. Scratch that. I did feel something. I felt peace."

"Where is your wife now," asked Zeke.

"No need to worry about her. She won't be nagging anyone else. Ever."

Myrna, knowing full well that Zeke had deployed a stall tactic, joined the conversation. "Why did you choose the victims? Did you know them?"

Zeke recognized Tony's anger but also the need for power. Both detectives know that serial killers select victims based on availability, vulnerability, and desirability.

"Of course not. I didn't really think much about them or killing. It was that young lady out in the storm that I realized I could do it. She just happened to be in the wrong place for what was going on in my head. After that, opportunities kept presenting itself. But then, I couldn't find anyone out and about like the first few, so I had to get creative. I went to the park to think, and that's when I saw the runner out in the rain as if he didn't have any damned sense."

"But why them?" Myrna pressed. "Why not those who got promoted over you? Or the ones promoting them?"

"Don't worry. Their turn is coming. All of them."

"How so?" Myrna continued.

"You'll find out soon enough.?

Zeke, understanding the delicate dance they were engaged in, appealed to Tony's ego. Anything to keep him calm. He complimented Tony's cunning, praising him for his ability to evade capture. However, he subtly introduced an element of doubt, insinuating that the only reason they even got close to uncovering his identity was through sheer chance.

"Well," said Zeke. You gave us a run for our money. I don't know if we would've ever caught you. We originally just wanted to talk with you due to the proximity of your work truck to two of the murders. Imagine our surprise to find you like this. Question: Did you make all of your guns?" asked Zeke.

"Sure did."

"Why use a different gun? Wouldn't it have been easier to just use the same one?" asked Myrna.

"That would have been the easy way. Yes. However, using the same gun would allude to one killer. The same killer."

"I understand the different gun approach, but why make your own guns? Isn't it time-consuming?" asked Zeke.

"Not as long as you think. My ghost gunner never sleeps. Never gets tired. It works when I'm at work and when I'm asleep. Purchasing a gun creates a greater chance that its striation fingerprint would be in IBIS. But you already know this, don't you? One gun for each job, and no one is the wiser." A few moments of silence passed.

"Well, that should be just enough time for the neighbors to get out of harm's way. We all know how this is going to end."

All eyes remain fixed on Tony's hands—the one resting on the remote and the other on the gun trigger. Myrna sensed the impasse and the dire consequences of any misstep. The conversation continued, with Tony expressing regret that he didn't have the opportunity to kill more, especially his boss, adding another layer of complexity to the already tense situation.

As the detectives attempted to navigate the delicate negotiations, Tony abruptly announced that their time together was coming to an end. The room fell silent as he pressed the button on the remote a split-second before pulling the trigger. The resounding blast of the Desert Eagle filled the basement, the massive round expanding instantly, tearing through the top of Tony's head and sending a gruesome spray of blood, bone fragments, and brain matter across the ceiling.

Myrna and Zeke instinctively flinched, assuming a standing fetal position posture as they braced for the imminent explosion they had feared. After a few heart-pounding moments, they cautiously stood up, exchanging a look of disbelief. Without hesitation, they raced for the exit, driven by the urgency to escape the potential blast radius.

# 36 | THIRTYSIX

Unbeknownst to the detectives or the unsuspecting residents, Tony's seemingly harmless press of the remote sent a clandestine signal to the substation on the outskirts of town. In response, the substation, like a dormant beast awakened from its slumber, unleashed a torrential surge of electricity, a potent cocktail of increased voltage and amperage, coursing through the power lines. This surge, normally tempered by transformers, now bypassed their protective barriers, hurtling unchecked toward the 4,714 homes tethered to its grid. The sudden influx of power moved swiftly, an invisible menace traveling silently through the veins of the electrical network.

As the overwhelming voltage surged through the unsuspecting homes, the dormant threat of electrical fires and shocks loomed large. While some electronic devices could withstand the onslaught, others stood vulnerable, their circuits overheating and igniting into flames. The surge protectors, usually a reliable line of defense, failed under the relentless pressure. In a deadly dance of destruction, the overloaded electrical currents sparked fires in homes ill-prepared for the sudden onslaught. The surge tripped breakers and blew fuses, but the excessive power continued to find paths through the electrical systems, wreaking havoc wherever it went.

The first flicker of danger manifested slowly as wisps of smoke curled from the windows of one unfortunate home. A toaster left plugged in began to smolder, its internal wiring melting and charring.

Then, like a morbid symphony, the flames from another home awakened. The short-circuit in a living room television set caused sparks to leap onto the nearby drapes, igniting them in an instant. Each ignition is a testament to Tony's unwitting sabotage. Within moments, the tranquil suburban street transformed into a scene of pandemonium as billowing smoke and crackling flames consumed the once-peaceful homes.

# 37 | THIRTYSEVEN

Myrna and Zeke maintained a vigilant watch from a safe distance outside the calculated blast radius, their eyes fixed on Tony's house. The bomb squad, officially known as Explosive Ordnance Disposal (EOD), deployed their arsenal of high-tech tools with precision and caution. Among their arsenal, the Remote-Controlled Vehicle (RCV), fondly nicknamed "The Wheelbarrow," deftly navigated the interior of the house. Equipped with microphones, cameras, sensors, and x-ray capabilities, it meticulously scoured for any signs of explosive devices or munitions.

The orchestrated scene unfolded with bomb-sniffing dogs, drones, and various other robotics joining the intricate dance of surveillance. Endoscope inspection cameras delved into hidden corners, leaving no nook or cranny unexamined. The EOD team, clad in formidable bomb protection suits resembling over-dressed versions of Marvel Comics' Juggernaut but in dark blue, stood poised for action. Their collective focus was on the readiness to respond if any trace of a bomb emerged during the search.

With methodical precision, they extended their scrutiny to the car and motorcycle parked in front of the suspect's house. Every precaution was taken to ensure a thorough investigation of the entire premises. The air around the scene buzzed with tension as each member of the team understood the gravity of their mission. The rhythmic hum of their equipment, the beeping of detectors, and the soft commands exchanged between team members added a soundtrack to the intense operation.

After an exhaustive hour of meticulous examination, the EOD team signaled the all-clear. Myrna, ever the impatient investigator, wasted no time in approaching the busy team leader, interrupting the careful stowing of devices, gadgets, and equipment. "What did you find?" she inquired, her determination evident, her tone demanding an immediate and thorough answer.

"Nothing," the EOD leader responded, his expression neutral but exhausted.

"Nothing?" Myrna pressed for clarification, her brow furrowing in disbelief.

"Correct. Nada, zilch, nicht, nothing," he reiterated, affirming the absence of any explosive materials, gunpowder, or detonators in the house. "The only thing we found were several boxes of various handgun ammunition neatly stacked in a corner of the basement.

Unconvinced, Myrna probed further. "What about the remote he had?" she asked, her tone tinged with skepticism and frustration.

"Not sure, but it's definitely a transmitter of sorts. It could be a remote for anything from a TV to a garage opener or an air conditioner to a stereo. It does have a range amplifier, so whatever it is controlling could be up to five miles away. I could track it, but it only has an encoder used to send a signal but lacks a decoder and receiver that receives and interprets the signal," the EOD leader explained, his technical jargon doing little to assuage Myrna's growing concern.

Finally satisfied with the investigation's outcome, Myrna allowed the matter to rest momentarily. However, lingering questions danced in her mind. "*Why would he tell us there's a bomb? What's the purpose?*" she mused, pondering the suspect's motives. "*What was he using the remote for?*" Her mind raced through possibilities, each more troubling than the last.

With the bomb threat dispelled, the scene transitioned to the arrival of forensics and the medical examination team. Despite Myrna's opinion of the cause of death, the investigation and examination would still have to go on. The forensics team moved in with the same precision and care as the EOD, their tasks equally critical.

Myrna stood amid her thoughts, grappling with the unsettling implications of the mysterious remote control. Her reverie was abruptly shattered by the crackle of her radio coming to life. The sudden burst of sound pierced the silence, filling the air with urgent voices tinged with panic.

"10-82, 10-82! We have multiple 10-82s in the Lanter Subdivision. Request fire and all available officers." The voice on the radio was frantic, the urgency of the situation unmistakable.

The cryptic message echoed through the receiver, its urgency sending a chill down Myrna's spine. She knew all too well what "10-82" signified in the coded language of emergency responders—a fire in progress. But the mention of "multiple 10-82s" painted a grim picture, indicating that not just one, but several blazes were raging through a residential community.

As the weight of the situation settled upon her, Myrna felt a sinking sensation in the pit of her stomach. The pieces of the puzzle began to fall into place with alarming clarity. The remote control, seemingly innocuous at first glance, now emerged as a sinister tool in a larger scheme of destruction. Its purpose was no longer a mystery—it had been the trigger for the fires now consuming the Lanter Subdivision.

With a sense of dread gnawing at her, Myrna realized the gravity of the situation. She would bet her career that Tony had unleashed a wave of chaos and devastation, using the remote control as a catalyst for igniting multiple fires across the community. The implications were chilling, hinting at a meticulously orchestrated plan aimed at sowing fear and destruction. Myrna entered the house, knowing that her dead killer was still killing.

# 38 | THIRTYEIGHT

The atmosphere outside Kathy's medical examination office was fraught with tension as Zeke ended a call with Derrick. Myrna, standing beside him, waited for the update on Tony's truck. Zeke, with a furrowed brow, delivered the unsettling news. He revealed that a disturbing discovery had been made regarding the control protection system.

Zeke's words hung heavy in the air, each syllable dripping with a mixture of urgency and concern as he delivered his unsettling report. "The utility workers stumbled upon remote devices hidden in at least a dozen substations. Each one was scheduled to go off at different pre-programmed times," he revealed, his tone laced with gravity. "The good news is that they were able to disable and disconnect them. However, and you already know this, Tony was the one who orchestrated the fires in the housing development that burned 1,300 houses to the ground."

The enormity of the destruction weighed heavily on Myrna as she absorbed the grim details. "How many homes did the substation serve?" she inquired, her voice tinged with disbelief.

"Derrick estimates it at a little over 4,700 residences," Zeke replied, his expression reflecting a mixture of shock and grim realization. "It's a miracle that more weren't burned down. The fact that the fires occurred when people were at work saved a lot of lives. The people who were at home were at least awake."

"But there's more, right?" asked Myrna, her brow furrowing with concern.

Zeke nodded solemnly. "Indeed. The neighborhoods he targeted were no random choices. It housed the residences of numerous executives from the electric company. And as if that wasn't enough, the other substations with the remote devices supplied power to the neighborhoods of those executives who didn't reside in the one that burned down."

"So, he DID go after those at his job after all. I guess that's what he meant when he said that their time will come," stated Myrna matter-of-factly.

"Yep," replied Zeke, "but most of them were spared since they found the devices at the other substations."

Myrna's frustration simmered beneath the surface, a potent mix of anger and sorrow for those whose lives had been needlessly shattered by one man's vengeful rampage. "It's infuriating," she seethed, her words punctuated by a clenched fist. "What the hell is wrong with him? These people didn't deserve to die, and their homes certainly didn't deserve to be razed to the ground. If his life was that bad, why didn't he just go out into the woods and kill himself instead of creating all this chaos, death and destruction?"

Zeke, ever the voice of reason amidst the chaos, offered a pragmatic perspective. "Apparently, hell hath no fury like an employee scorned, but there's always the option of seeking professional help," he suggested, his tone tempered by a sense of pragmatism.

Myrna's response was swift and vehement. "Professional help?" she scoffed incredulously. "Do you honestly believe that twisted minds like his would willingly seek redemption? In his mind, there's nothing wrong with him. How would you convince him otherwise? No, they'd rather play the blame game, casting themselves as the victims of circumstance while inflicting untold suffering upon the innocent."

Zeke nodded in somber agreement, his features etched with a shared sense of grief and resolve. "We're in complete accord on that front," he acknowledged. "I guess the question becomes how does one convince someone like him that something is wrong when he truly believes that he's done nothing wrong? Like, how do you convince a fool that they're a fool? Or a know-it-all that they're wrong?"

Myrna slowly shook her head. "I wish I knew."

"You and me both," sighed Zeke. "Let's see what Kathy has for us."

Kate greeted them with a warm smile as they entered her office. It's a welcome respite from the grim realities they just finished addressing.

"Hey, Myrna. Zeke." The detectives provided a silent nod. "So," said Kathy, "I was going through the personal effects of your perp, and I found something interesting in his pocket."

With a sense of trepidation, Myrna broached the subject of the killer's personal effects, her curiosity mingling with a hint of apprehension. "Like what?" asked Myrna.

"A letter," replied Kathy.

"What kind of letter?" asked Zeke.

"I'm not exactly sure how to answer that."

"What do you mean," chimed Myrna. "Who's it addressed to?"

"Well, it would appear that it is addressed to the two of you." Kathy's reply was cryptic as she handed over the ominous missive.

---------------------------------------------------

Dear Detectives (whoever you are):

If you're reading this, it's because I decided to let you live to do so. I could have easily taken it. Remember that as you go about each and every one of your days for the rest of your life. Although I am gone, I will forever live on in your head because I am the one who spared your life. What will you do with the gift I have given you?

Tony

P.S. Gone, but STILL in control.

---------------------------------------------

The detectives absorbed the chilling words of the letter. Myrna couldn't help but express her disdain for the twisted mind behind the letter. "He should've 'taken control' of his own life a long time ago. If he did, all his victims would still be alive."

Kind of makes you think, though, huh?" asked Kathy as the detectives looked up from the letter. Both Myrna and Zeke, unable to meet her gaze, shifted their focus downward, contemplating the weight of Tony's words. Unbeknownst to each other, Myrna and Zeke embarked on a silent introspection, mentally taking stock of their lives.

# 39 | THIRTYNINE

Myrna and Zeke shuffled through the parking lot outside the Medical Examiner's office building. The late afternoon sun stretched its weary light across the asphalt, casting elongated shadows that clung to the ground. The air hung heavy, thick with the unvoiced weight of everything that had unfolded that day. The last few water spots and puddles lingered from what the weather forecast said was the last storm of tornado season. Zeke, breaking the heavy silence that had settled between them, asked, "Whatcha tinkin' 'bout?" His voice was casual, but his eyes were sharp, studying his partner closely, trying to read the emotions she was trying to hide.

After a moment, Myrna, without looking up, muttered, "Nothing. Why?" Her voice was distant, and she kept her gaze fixed on the ground, avoiding eye contact.

"Jus askin'," Zeke replied, though he knew she was lying. He was not sure what was on her mind, but he knew something had rattled her. After all, they had been working together for nearly two decades, and he could read her like a book. He sensed the turmoil beneath her calm facade, the way she tightened her jaw and the slight furrow in her brow.

"Yeah, I'm good. Just thinking," Myrna said, her voice lacking conviction. She kicked a loose pebble across the lot, watching it skitter away.

"Bout?" Zeke probed gently, hoping she'll open up. His concern for her was genuine, and he wished she would let him in on whatever was troubling her.

"Just life. In general," she responded, her tone clipped and uninviting. She shoved her hands into her pockets, feeling the cool metal of her keys against her fingertips.

Both detectives were visibly uncomfortable, the unspoken tension between them growing thicker with each passing second. Zeke knew better than to push too hard, so he decided to let it go for now. The asphalt underfoot felt hot, almost sticky, as the late summer sun bared down on them, making the air shimmer with heat.

Zeke's phone chirped, breaking the uncomfortable silence. He glanced at the screen and said, "Saved by the bell." The relief in his voice is conspicuous, giving him an excuse to escape the awkward moment.

"Yep," Myrna replied, her voice flat and distant.

"I have to take off," Zeke said, heading toward his Batmobile. He gave her a quick nod, hoping she'd be okay.

"Batman has a date?" Myrna asked, trying to lighten the mood, but her attempt fell flat. She forced a smile, but it didn't reach her eyes.

Zeke shook his head and waved her off as he walked away. As he entered the car, Myrna laughingly yelled, "You didn't say no."

Zeke drove off, leaving Myrna alone in the parking lot. She watched him go, feeling a strange mix of relief and loneliness. Once the car was out of sight, she let out a deep sigh that had been seemingly building up for over a decade. The weight of her thoughts pressed down on her, making her feel both weary and restless.

Myrna walked slowly toward her own car, the sound of her footsteps echoing in the quiet parking lot. She fumbled with her keys, her mind racing with thoughts she couldn't quite pin down. Images of the latest case, the faces of the victims, and snippets of old conversations with Zeke swirl in her mind, blending into a chaotic storm of emotions.

She got into her car but didn't start the engine right away. Instead, she sat there, gripping the steering wheel tightly as if trying to anchor herself in the present. Her eyes wandered to the rearview mirror, catching a glimpse of her own reflection. She looked tired, the lines on her face etched deeper than she remembered. The years had taken their toll, and the weight of countless cases seemed to have settled into her bones.

Myrna's thoughts drifted to her family, the strained relationship with her mother, and the absence of her father. The unresolved issues and unspoken words weighed heavily on her, adding to the burden she carried daily. She wondered if she would ever find the peace she so desperately needed. The memories of her father flashed before her eyes—his smile, his words of wisdom, and the void his absence had left.

A gentle breeze stirred outside, rustling the leaves of a nearby tree. Myrna took a deep breath, trying to find some semblance of calm amidst the turmoil. She knew she had to keep going, had to keep pushing forward, but in this moment, she allowed herself to feel the weight of it all. For a woman who rarely cried, her chest tightened from the pressure of the emotions she had kept bottled up for too long. And finally, she wept.

# 40 | FORTY
# EPILOGUE ONE

In the softly lit hospital room, Mrs. Cortes swiped at her phone. The device became both a source of distraction and a lifeline to the outside world. She paused intermittently between swipes; her gaze drifted toward the wall a few feet from the foot of the hospital bed. There, she contemplated the unknown, lost in her own thoughts. Brief moments of stillness were punctuated by prolonged breaks, during which she placed the phone down, allowing her eyes to wander into the distance or fixate on the ceiling when her head leaned back on the inclined bed. The beeping of the medical equipment provided a rhythmic backdrop to her introspection, a constant reminder of her current reality.

A pained smile graced her face as she delicately positioned her cell phone on the mobile bedside table, slightly adjusting the bed for comfort. She was not exactly a young woman anymore. The recent surgery reminded her should she forget. She was making strides, but she was still tender, especially around the fresh four-inch scar on the lower right-hand side of her abdomen.

The room remained hushed, filled only with the rhythmic beeping of medical equipment and the occasional soft hum from the air conditioning vent. The white walls were bare except for a small, generic painting of a serene landscape. Its presence did little to alleviate the sterile ambiance of the room.

An unexpected knock on the door jolted Mrs. Cortes out of her contemplative state. Startled, she managed a weak "yes?" into the empty room. Silence followed, leaving her to murmur, "Oh, well." Finally, the door opened, and a voice broke the quietude.

"Hello, Mrs. Cortes. How are you feeling?"

Mrs. Cortes craned her neck upward to take in Zeke's full height. "Um, I've been better, I suppose. Um, are you new? What happened to Dr...?"

"Oh. I'm sorry. My name is Zeke."

"Dr. Zeke? That's an interesting last name."

Zeke chuckled heartily, bringing a touch of warmth into the room. "No, ma'am. Zeke is my first name. Well...sort of. Let me start again. My name is Detective Ezekial LaPorte. My friends call me Zeke."

"Detective? What's a detective doing here?"

The mention of 'detective' caused her to sit up abruptly. Concern and a sharp pain etched across her face. "Oh, no. Is...is Myrna okay?"

"Huh? Oh. Of course. Of course. I'm so sorry. Yes, Myrna is okay. I didn't mean to worry you." Relief washed over her face.

"I just wanted you to know that Myrna is really trying to have a relationship with you. But she's not good at this sort of thing. She's also impatient. And although she would never mention it, she longs to connect with you."

"No need to worry about that. She probably won't be back here anyhow. She hates me, you know."

Zeke offered a reassuring smile. "That's not true at all, Mrs. Cortes. She just needs a little time. She'll come around. She has so many things on her heart."

"Like what?" Mrs. Cortes asked, her curiosity piqued.

"Well, for one, she misses her dad."

"Yeah. I miss him, too. Very much. He always knew exactly what to say or do and when to do it. They were like two peas in a pod, and I always felt like an outcast. I always felt like I had to compete for their attention."

"That's interesting you say that because that is exactly how Myrna feels. She's an accomplished detective in a major city, but she feels like it still isn't enough for you to say that you're proud of her. You think that she hates you, and funny enough, she thinks that you hate her."

"What? She's my daughter. I could never hate her. And I am proud of her."

"You know that. I even know that. At least I do now. But unfortunately, she doesn't."

Mrs. Cortes sat in silence, taking in all that Zeke had shared. The weight of his words settled heavily on her, mingling with her own thoughts and emotions.

Zeke stood. "I have to run, Mrs. Cortes. It was a pleasure meeting you. By the way, if you could, would you keep my little visit just between us? I wouldn't want to worry, Myrna."

"Sure," she replied softly.

"Remember what I said."

"Okay. I will. You must be a good friend to her. I try my best."

Zeke opened the door just as a visitor pushed in. "Oops. I'm so sorry," he said.

"What are you doing here?" Myrna's voice is sharp, edged with confusion and irritation.

"Oh. Hey, Myrna. I was just leaving."

"You still didn't answer my question," Myrna insisted, her eyes narrowing as she studied him.

"Oh. I didn't?"

"No. You didn't."

"Listen, Myrna. You're a great detective. You're also a good, caring person. You just have a different way of showing it. But you have to know it, even if no one else does, regardless of what others think. It starts with you. In the words of Marcus Aurelius, 'It never ceases to amaze me that we love ourselves more than other people but care more about their opinion than our own.' You can do this. I believe in you." Zeke's tone was sincere, his words meant to reassure and empower.

With glistened eyes, Myrna smiled and nodded. She wiped at her eyes and, with a slightly strained voice, said, "You still didn't answer my question."

Zeke's smile deepened. "I know." He placed a gentle paw of a hand on his partner's shoulder and guided her into the room. The door began to close softly behind him, leaving Myrna alone with her mother. As the door finally closed, he heard Myrna take a deep breath and say, "Hi, Mom. Can we talk?"

# 41 | FORTYONE
# EPILOGUE TWO

The jet-black car rested like a silent sentinel at the edge of the cul-de-sac in the tranquil residential community. Its sleek exterior gleamed faintly under the glow of the moon, betraying no hint of the turmoil brewing within its driver's mind. Behind the tinted windows, the driver sat in an eerie stillness, his thoughts swirling tumultuously as he grappled with the weight of his decision. The night air is still, the silence punctuated only by the occasional rustling of leaves or distant hum of nocturnal creatures.

Contemplation wrestled with determination as the driver stared at the rancher looming ahead. He knew what he must do and rehearsed it countless times in his mind, yet doubt gnaws at the edges of his resolve. With a trembling hand, he reached for the ignition start button, fingers hovering hesitantly before retreating, the moment of reckoning postponed once more. His breathing was shallow, each breath a struggle against the anxiety threatening to overwhelm him.

Summoning his courage, he emerged from the car, his footsteps measured and deliberate on the pavement. The warm night air brushed against his skin, a stark contrast to the coolness inside the vehicle. A brief touch to the holster at his hip reassured him, but he decided against the weapon, tucking it away in the confines of the vehicle's secure center console. The choice made, he locked the car in silence and embarked on his clandestine mission. His heart pounded in his chest; each beat was a reminder of the stakes involved.

As he approached the rancher, the serenity of the night was pierced by the soft glow emanating from the large window. Muffled voices drifted through the stillness, accompanied by the intermittent hum of a television set. His gaze lingered on the small green glow by the door— an electronic doorbell, a sentinel of modern technology poised to betray his presence. He took a deep breath, steeling himself for the task ahead.

Undeterred, he moved with painstaking slowness, mindful of the motion sensors that could betray him. He knew the dangers of the advanced surveillance systems, yet his determination outweighed his apprehension. With each cautious step, he inched closer to his target, his heart pounding in his chest. The familiar ache of fear gnawed at him, but he pushed it aside, focusing on his objective.

At last, he reached the front door, his hand hovering over the knob. To his surprise, it yielded easily under his touch, confirming his suspicions that the door was unlocked. With bated breath, he pushed the door open, the hinges protesting softly against the intrusion. He slipped inside, closing the door with a barely audible click. The dim interior was a stark contrast to the bright moonlit exterior, shadows playing across the walls and floor.

Before he could fully orient himself within the dim interior, a movement caught his attention—a shadow dancing across the floor. His muscles tensed, anticipation thrumming through his veins as he braced for confrontation. He scanned the room quickly, taking in the familiar yet altered surroundings. The air inside was heavy with anticipation as if the house itself was holding its breath.

Suddenly, a voice breaks the silence, an unexpected sound echoing through the house. "Zeke," it called out, a note of relief coloring the tone. "You made it." The voice is familiar, stirring a mix of emotions within him.

Startled, the intruder froze, his gaze locked onto the figure before him. At that moment, amidst the uncertainty and danger, a glimmer of recognition sparked within him—a connection forged in the crucible of shared history and unforeseen circumstances.

"I knew you would come," the figure continued, stepping into the light. The face was worn but kind, eyes reflecting a complex blend of relief and worry.

"Surprise," replied a reluctant Zeke, his voice tinged with a mix of emotions he struggles to suppress. The tension in the room eased slightly, replaced by a fragile sense of understanding.

Before he could say another word, Dominick had already embraced him. The hug was unexpected, a surge of warmth and familiarity in a situation fraught with tension. Hesitantly, Zeke hugged him back. The embrace was tentative at first, then grew stronger, as if both were seeking solace and reassurance in the connection.

The room seemed to exhale, the heavy atmosphere lightening as the two stood together. Dominick pulled back slightly and looked into Zeke's eyes with a mixture of gratitude and apology. "I didn't know if you'd come. But I hoped."

Zeke nodded, the words catching in his throat. "I almost didn't," he admitted, his voice barely above a whisper. The truth of his statement hung between them, a testament to the internal battle he had fought to get here. Dominick guided Zeke further into the house, the familiar surroundings taking on a new significance.

# PLEASE LEAVE A REVIEW

*If you enjoyed Serial Rain, it would mean a lot to Jameo if you were able to leave a review. Reviews are an important way for books to find new readers.*

*Thank you*

# About the Author

Welcome to Jameo's world of words! Jameo (JAY-me-oh) Pollock is a suspense thriller author known for weaving suspenseful, fast-paced thrillers that keep readers on the edge of their seats. A lifelong storyteller, Jameo has always been fascinated by the darker side of human nature, blending intricate plots with complex, flawed characters.

With a background in learning and development, Jameo brings a sharp eye for detail and a love for mystery to every book. He holds a Doctorate of Education in Global Training and Human Performance Improvement, a master's Degree in Adult Education & Curriculum Development, and a BBA in Management and Finance.

When he's not lost in the realm of fiction, you can find him cycling, reading, meditating, playing video games, and taking pictures, all of which often inspire elements of his novels.

Jameo is a combat veteran of the United States Army and lives in Virginia. His work has been praised for its unexpected twists, gripping narratives, rich character development, and vivid imagery.

This is Jameo's second novel in the genre, and he looks forward to continuing to captivate readers with more thrilling stories to come.

You can connect with Jameo at www.jameopollock.com or at the following social media sites.

Facebook: Author Jameo Pollock

Instagram: www.instagram.com/jameopollock/

YouTube: https://www.youtube.com/@dr.jameopollock

# MEDICAL SILENCE:
## A Myrna Sontiago Novella Series
### (Coming Soon)

In the dimly lit chamber, shadows danced along the walls, casting ominous shapes that flickered in the sparse light. It was eerily silent. The silence was shattered only by the muffled, sinister words emanating from behind a foreboding mask. The figure loomed menacingly over the immobilized figure strapped to the gurney. The air was thick with dread as the masked figure's voice sliced through the stillness, each word dripping with malice. "I know you can't speak, but I know you can hear me," the voice echoed.

The victim, rendered helpless from an unknown substance coursing through his veins, lay in silence. "You're paralyzed, but you can still feel pain. And pain you will feel. It's time for you to pay for what you did."

The figure stood and double-checked the respirator mask over the face of the motionless body. "I'm certain you have many questions. But just know that you've been very bad, and it's time for you to pay for what you did."

"This room is designed for two things," they declared with twisted pride. "One is to keep you alive long enough for me to accomplish my mission." The victim's eyes, the only part of the body still under their control, widened in horror as the full extent of his predicament dawned upon him. "The second is to provide some privacy while I do my work."

"The ventilator, that mask on your face, is to force air into and out of your lungs," the tormentor explained, their voice dripping with sadistic glee. "You see, the cocktail I administered to you paralyzes your muscles, up to and including your diaphragm."

"Once it stops, you stop, if you catch my drift," the masked figure chuckled darkly, reveling in the victim's terror. "So, this ventilator is going to keep you alive while I administer your punishment."

"Oh, I forgot to mention," the tormentor added casually as if discussing the weather, "the cocktail doesn't block your pain receptors. And, as I mentioned earlier, you will feel everything."

"Then, once I'm done with you," the masked figure concluded with chilling finality, "I'll remove the ventilator and allow you to die like the sorry dog that you are."

The figure picked up a dull metal punch tool and placed the narrow end near the victim's left eye socket. "I suppose I'll start by breaking your orbital bone. Holding the punch steady, the figure slowly raised a ball peen hammer, preparing to strike the punch.

"Shhhh. Don't say a word."

# Back Cover

Amid a torrential thunderstorm, a murderer descends upon Dallas.

After the first body is found, it seems the rain will never stop. Then another body is found. One for each thunderstorm, and this is the rainy season.

As panic grips the city, detectives Myrna Sontiago and Zeke LaPorte are tasked with bringing an end to the bloodshed.

With rainy-day murders and washed-out crime scenes, the detectives are faced with one looming question: How do you catch a killer with no evidence?

Unputdownable and packed with twists and turns, this suspense thriller will forever change the way you think about the rain.

Serial Rain is a gripping novella that weaves together elements of mystery, suspense, and psychological intrigue.

From the author of the debut novella Mirrored Echoes, who has a knack for creating vivid imagery and tension.